W9-CTK-299

DATE DUE

AUG 1 5 1989	
AUG 27 1994	
SEP - 3 2002	

BRODART, INC.   Cat. No. 23-221

THE LION'S CUB

The following names have been changed since the
time of Czar Nicholas I

Then	Now
TIFLIS	TBILSI
VLADIKAVKAZ	ORDZHANIKIDZE
ST. PETERSBURG	LENINGRAD

*The highest peak in the Caucasus Mountains is
Mt. El'Bruz, with an elevation of 18,510 feet.*

H. M. HOOVER

THE LION'S CUB

FOUR WINDS PRESS   NEW YORK

J

Library of Congress Cataloging in Publication Data
Hoover, H. M.
    The Lion's cub.
    SUMMARY: Describes the changes that take place
in the life of a Caucasus chieftain's son before and during
his stay as a hostage in the court of Nicholas I.
    [1. Caucasus—History—Fiction. 2. Russia—History—
19th century—Fiction] I. Title.
PZ7.H7705Li   [Fic]   74–8594
ISBN 0–590–07375–3

PUBLISHED BY FOUR WINDS PRESS
A DIVISION OF SCHOLASTIC MAGAZINES, INC., NEW YORK, N.Y.
COPYRIGHT © 1974 BY H. M. HOOVER
ALL RIGHTS RESERVED
PRINTED IN THE UNITED STATES OF AMERICA
LIBRARY OF CONGRESS CATALOG CARD NUMBER: 74–8594
1   2   3   4   5   78   77   76   75   74

TO ROSE AND TEDDY

HISTORICAL NOTES

THE STORY OF JEMAL-EDIN IS LESS THAN A FOOTNOTE TO THE long forgotten Wars of the Caucasus (1800–1859). In the pages of history Jemal-Edin is overshadowed by the towering and often terrible figures of two men: his father, Shamil, and the man whose ward he became, Czar Nicholas I.

When Russia moved eastward in her period of great colonial expansion, she encountered little prolonged resistance until reaching the mountain of Daghestan. Here the Caucasus, the mountain chain stretching from the Caspian to the Black Sea, separated what was then the Christian world from the Moslem, Arab from Infidel, Cross from Crescent.

The Caucasus has a history of bloodshed that continues into our own time. Throughout the centuries the ferocity of the mountain tribes had repelled invaders. The Persians, Alexander the Great, the legions of Rome, Genghis Khan, Attila the Hun—all met defeat in these mountains. And when the mountaineers were not fighting invaders, they fought among themselves for the sheer joy of it. Feuds and vendettas decimated whole generations of families. War was a sport, vengeance a duty.

Russia was determined to conquer the Caucasus and thus achieve her dream of opening an overland route to India. Just as determined to keep her from doing this was the Imam Shamil. He declared Holy War and welded together the separately warring Moslem tribes in the mountains to his cause.

THE LION'S CUB

ON THE FIFTH MORNING OF JUNE THE ELITE HOST OF
the Murid army rode forth from the village of Dargo.
At the army's head rode Shamil, Imam of Daghestan.
He was mounted on the finest of Kabardian stallions.
The horse was black, its saddle soft crimson, and its
trappings of tooled silver. For in Daghestan, Shamil
was ruler of both church and state, a priest-king.
There were none higher than he.

In the square before the mosque and overflowing
into the surrounding narrow streets, the warriors assembled to leave. On the flat rooftops old men and
children clustered to cheer the army farewell. Half-
starved dogs raced under the horses and yipped in
excitement. From behind the rugs that screened
doorways veiled women peered out at the riders.

A cry went up from among the mounted men. *"La
Allah illa Allahai!* There is no god but Allah! There is
no Imam but Shamil Imam!" Shamil raised his arm.

1

Silence fell. Above the sound of the wind buffeting across the mountain came the shriek of the massive gate of iron and logs scraping over the stones.

Jemal-Edin, Shamil's first-born son and heir, stood in the wind atop the wall by the gate and watched the army leave. Although it was the largest army ever assembled in his village, the boy had eyes only for his father. For even among the most faithful of his followers, there was none who worshipped the Imam more than this son.

At dawn, in the mosque, Jemal-Edin had knelt on the prayer rug beside his father to join their prayers to Allah. He had heard Shamil's invocation to the Lord Allah to grant the Murid army victory over the Infidels. "The swish of the sword of the Lord Allah on the necks of unbelievers is pious and righteous!" quoted Shamil. It was his belief and that of his people that instant death was the just fate due any Russian or Cossack who threatened the independence of their mountain land.

Cold gray clouds from the Caspian Sea shrouded the peaks above the village. Snow had fallen during the night. Its whiteness cloaked the boxlike houses that clung to the cliffside, softened their flat roofs, and capped the spired minaret with a crystal fringe.

Shamil barked the command to move out. Standing upright in the stirrups, heedless of the slippery snow, he gave the stallion a cut with the whip so that it reared high. Forcing the horse to wheel, he galloped at top speed toward the gate in the wall. Then, within an inch of being beheaded by the stone cross-bar, he slung himself sideways, still erect, nearly beneath the horse's belly.

The people cheered wildly.

Fifteen yards on the other side of the gate, the bluff on which the village stood ended on a cliff. Hundreds of feet below lay a ravine spiked with jagged stones. At the cliff's edge Shamil reared and wheeled his stallion again, making a sharp left turn to gallop down the narrow path along the precipice, the hoofs of his horse striking sparks as they pounded over the snowy rock.

Although Jemal-Edin had seen his father ride out like this dozens of times before, still his heart stopped beating for a moment. Behind Shamil came his officers, dressed in black and mounted on black stallions like their leader. The warriors followed, dark and eagle-faced, hard and slim as dancers. Like Shamil they took the path at breakneck speed, though not so recklessly as he.

And when all had cleared the gate, the men began to sing. Their voices raised in a battle song that echoed and re-echoed through the mountain ravines. The banners of war floated black against the spring snow. Their sabers glittered in the cold morning light.

"Ho, the Chosen of Allah," they sang, "there is no fear upon them, nor do they grieve." And when the villagers who watched heard this chant, some made their own prayer. For their army rode to Akhulgo, the village whose name meant "a place for meeting in time of danger." Toward Akhulgo, from the opposite direction, marched the main force of the Russian army.

Even the children knew it was a time of grave danger for the mountain people. For the past year massive Russian forces had been making successful advances. Village upon village fell before the Infidels' might. Tribe after tribe of once brave warriors surrendered in shame to gold-braided generals. Rumors of massacres and butchery raced through the rock canyons. Now the Russians threatened the very heart of Daghestan where the tribes most faithful to Shamil continued to resist conquest.

As winter relaxed its grip on the high country, the Russians had followed the spring ever upwards, conquering everything in their wake. Four Russian armies, each coming from a different direction, were closing in on Shamil's stronghold of Akhulgo, attempting to encircle his fierce Murid warriors and, by one final battle, end a war which had begun when Jemal-Edin's grandmother was a child.

It was a fact accepted by all, no matter what their age, that if the Murids were to lose this battle at Akhulgo, all would die fighting—if they were lucky. For if they did not die in battle, then they believed they would become the slaves of the Russians, and the proud Murids preferred death to such dishonor.

Jemal-Edin watched and listened until the last rider had disappeared into the misty clouds drifting over the mountain and the last of the song echoed from the rocks. Then he sighed. Once again he had been left behind.

"It will be a dark time for me and for my people

when I must risk the life of my first-born son before he is truly a man," Shamil had said in response to Jemal-Edin's plea to accompany him. "For now it is Allah's wish and my command that you remain in Dargo. It may be that I shall need you at Akhulgo. If that should come to pass, I will send for you. Until then, you will obey my command."

But Jemal-Edin knew why he had been left behind. It was because his father thought the village of Dargo was so remote that it would not be threatened by the sweep of the Russian army. Like all the women and children staying here, he was being protected from danger. It was a galling thought.

He could ride as well as any warrior and fire a rifle as accurately. With his saber he could cut down a two-inch thick sapling in one stroke. He could creep up on the wily mountain marmots without their hearing a thing and kill them with one swift throw of his dagger. They would be dead before they could so much as whistle a warning to their neighbors.

Shamil knew this and was proud of his son's prowess. Still he would not be swayed.

As Jemal-Edin turned to climb down off the wall, the boys beside him stepped back respectfully to give him room. The son of the Imam must be shown the same respect as the Imam himself. So Shamil had decreed. But it was these signs of respect that made his son so impatient to become a man. It set him apart from the other boys, isolated him against his will, insured that everything he said or did was watched and reported upon.

In the schoolroom of the mosque he was expected

to know all the verses of the Koran. Was not his father Imam? When he dipped his brush into the ink to inscribe those same verses upon a scroll, both his penmanship and his Arabic must be classical and perfect. Was he not the son of the Imam? If other boys argued and fought among themselves, he could not. It would mean a loss of dignity to his father's name. And if, because he could not honorably escape doing so, he was forced to fight a boy; he had to win. Or his father's pride would suffer. The pride of the Imam Shamil the Avar, Lion of Daghestan, Leader of the Faithful of Allah, was great.

Sometimes it seemed to Jemal-Edin that he was always on the outside looking in, always lonely. And never more so than on this gray morning when his father rode away. The wind on the wall had chilled him through, and he shivered as he came down the stone steps and hurried toward his house.

It was only a little warmer inside the stone-and-log house than it was outside. Here, at least, the worst of the wind did not penetrate. A slave, a Turkish boy made captive on one of Shamil's raids, helped him off with his white goatskin cloak and then retreated backwards, eyes averted in respect, toward the door.

The boy's mother, Fatimat, Shamil's first wife, knelt before the fire putting skewered lamb shish kebab on the grate for his breakfast. Shamil had taken his chef with him to Akhulgo. She looked up at him as he entered the room, her eyes smiling above her veil. But she said nothing. Fatimat was a well-trained Avar woman; she spoke only when it was necessary to speak. She served him his breakfast and then she withdrew, going to her own apartment and leaving him to his own amusements.

The sheepskin curtain which served as a door between living and sleeping quarters was pushed aside. Kazi Mohammed came into the front room. Seeing his big brother sitting on the stool before the fire brought a shy pleased smile to the little boy's face. As Jemal-Edin worshipped his father, so Kazi Mohammed worshipped his older brother. He came over and sat at Jemal-Edin's feet.

"I saw our father leave," he announced proudly as he took the cube of lamb Jemal-Edin offered him. "I was standing up on the roof. Did you know the rafters shake when many horses gallop past?"

Jemal-Edin shook his head as he put the meat back over the smoky dung fire to cook more thoroughly.

"They do!" Kazi assured him. "When they come back you can come up there and stand with me—see for yourself!"

"They will not come back. Not for a long time."

"How do you know?" The little boy looked worried.

"I heard Father tell Mother. He said when they win at Akhulgo, he will drive the Infidels' army to the sea. He may be gone all summer—or longer."

Kazi Mohammed sighed. "I wish I could help fight the Infidels," he said wistfully.

Jemal-Edin nodded agreement. For a long moment the two brothers sat silently, wishing childhood's end, their right hands unconsciously gripping the hilt of the long dagger each wore at their belt. The lamb over the fire began to sputter and spit. Jemal-

Edin grabbed the skewer and waved it about to cool. The fat dripped over the hearthstone of the wide-mouthed fireplace. He deftly removed the first chunk with his teeth and handed the skewer to his brother.

"Do you want to go riding today?" Kazi Mohammed asked as he chewed. "If it clears off, we can take the falcon."

"The mollah wants us in class."

"Today?"

"Father ordered it."

Kazi Mohammed sighed again. The mollah was a holy man who taught what passed as school for the boys of the village. His classes consisted totally of religious instruction. In addition to the tenets of the Murid sect, the boys learned to read and write the classic Arabic script of the Koran. If they learned to count, it was by identifying verse and chapter of the Koran. Among themselves they spoke only the Avar language, although they could neither read nor write it. All practical education they were expected to learn from their elders. The fact that the mollah was an aged ascetic with little patience for the energy of boys and a tendency to use the horsewhip made his classes even less popular.

The mosque was cold. The nearly sixty boys in their wooly lambskin coats and hats sat on their prayer rugs, legs folded beneath them. Still the smaller boys shivered. Jemal-Edin would have liked to sit in the middle of the group where the bodies of the others provided some warmth against the icy drafts which swept over the stone floor and also served as shields from the wrath of the mollah. But Shamil's position decreed that his sons sit directly in front of the teacher, a spot no other boy envied.

Class began with a prayer for the victory of the Murid warriors against the Russian invaders. Then the mollah began explaining why ruthless war and violence were not at odds with the gentle teachings of the first Murid Imam, Mollah Mohammed.

"Our first Imam was a man of great peace," said the mollah. "He bore arms against no man. But our second Imam died under the guns of the Infidels. He was not allowed to follow the Path toward Truth. Now to live in peace means to submit to the Infidels' rule—to forsake our customs and our Faith. Until we have driven out the invaders there can be no peace! The Shariat, the Law for the guidance of all men as decreed by Allah and his Prophet Mohammed, remains unchanging and unchangeable. Nor has the Law changed. But The Path has! Now the Path to Paradise lies in the shadows of war!

"In a few years you yourselves will be men. To be a man is to be a warrior! Chaste and dedicated to the Cause of Holy War! Chaste and dedicated to Allah and to Allah's chosen, Shamil Imam, our ruler under Allah! So it is written! So it shall be!"

In spite of the fact that Jemal-Edin had heard much the same thing many times before, he found himself getting excited. It was true! In a few years he would be a man, a warrior. And as a warrior he would ride into battle at the right hand of Shamil. When he was experienced, he himself would lead men on raids

and sorties. It would be his voice that led the terrify-
ing war chant as a band of warriors swooped out of
the hills to pillage and burn a Russian or Cossack
settlement. His saber thrust would dispatch the
leader of a packtrain bound for Tiflis. His men would
bring home the captured booty of war! He would find
glory and pride in the eyes of his father! If only one
did not have to wait so long to grow up. What if the
war ended before he got to fight?

But in the days that followed, it seemed as if waiting was all anyone could do. Shamil had given orders
that no one was to leave the mountain until he gave
them permission to go. There were Russian troops
throughout the Caucasus in areas where they had
never before been. Shamil's spies reported that Dargo
did not appear on Russian military maps. The Imam
intended that it remain a secret village fortress.

The rain that followed the spring snow continued.
The stone streets became narrow streams which
washed the garbage toward the walls. Slaves were
sent out to sweep all of it out the gate and off the cliff.
The wide-chimneyed fireplaces smoked even more
than usual. The roofs of several houses collapsed, victims of the weather. Housewives brought into the
house those goats and sheep who had given birth, so
that the lambs and kids would survive the cold spring.

Jemal-Edin, his brother, and the other boys spent
most of their days in the now almost empty stables.
They played games and when that paled, groomed
the few horses left there or braided horsehair for rope
and halters.

When they grew too cold outside, the two boys would come home and go to their mother's rooms where she and Shamil's second wife, Javaret, sat all day at their looms weaving rugs. The boys would stretch out on the cushioned bench along the wall and watch the hands of the two women as they changed dyed wool into geometrics of great color and beauty. It was quiet there and peaceful. Sometimes the boys would fall asleep, but usually they listened. As they wove the two women would talk, telling stories of their childhood in distant villages.

Fatimat came from a noble family. Her father was a surgeon, the only one in the whole of Daghestan. She herself could read and write and was far more educated than most men of the Avar tribe. Fortunately, Shamil had overlooked that defect and married her because he loved her. Javaret was a girl of traditional upbringing. Her father was a chieftain. Shamil had married her because he wanted sons and to ally her father's tribe to his Cause of Holy War.

One dawn the rain ended. With it ended the waiting. For Shamil had sent his first officer, the noble Hassan, back to Dargo with four other warriors. He brought a message for Fatimat.

"It is the Imam's command that his family join him. You will be prepared to leave before dusk. Pack only food and clothing for the trip. We will be traveling by night over hidden trails."

When Jemal-Edin heard those words he could hardly contain his whoop for joy. They were going to

Akhulgo! He would be with his father in time of battle! He could not understand the look of concern on his mother's face as she listened.

"He wishes Javaret to come, too?"

Hassan nodded.

"But she is pregnant. She will have her child within the month."

"The Imam commanded that she accompany you."

Fatimat said nothing but her eyes narrowed above her veil. Hassan shifted uncomfortably. He never felt at ease with this wife of his master's. "It is the Imam's command," he repeated. If she refused to come, he would be punished.

"Very well. We shall be ready."

THEY LEFT IN THE AFTERNOON. HASSAN ORDERED
that, for the sake of security, they tell no one they
were going. Still word got about. As the small party
rode from the courtyard of Shamil's house by the
mosque, a murmur rose in the suddenly crowded
square. Shopkeepers appeared under their awnings;
veiled women paused to watch the caravan ride past
and yanked small children out of the path of the
horses.

There were no cheers now as there had been when
the army rode away. It was as if the whole village
suspected Shamil must be in great need if he sent for
his family at such a time. And the meaning implied in
their departure was sobering.

But not for Jemal-Edin. To him the whole thing
was exciting. Like any warrior riding out, his rifle
hung from his saddle. In the prayer rug rolled as a

saddle pack was a supply of food, dried meat, goat cheese, raisins, and dried apricots. He had polished his dagger until it gleamed in the sun. In his mind he was going to join his father in battle, and woe to the Infidel who crossed his path! The possibility of dying in battle never entered his mind.

He was mounted on Baba. Although technically a full-grown horse, Baba was hardly taller than the pony Kazi Mohammed rode. A Tartar horse, born wild and captured on one of Shamil's raids, Baba was small, black and shaggy, but very strong and sure-footed as a goat on the treacherous mountain paths.

The steward opened the great gate for the party and bowed as the family of the Imam passed through and turned down the trail. Hassan led the way. Behind him rode two warriors, then the women and children. Two more warriors followed, leading two packhorses that could also be used for riding in case one of the mounts went lame.

When they were halfway down the trail, on an impulse Jemal-Edin turned in his saddle and looked back on the village of Dargo. Dwarfed by the giant peaks above it, it huddled behind its walls on the ridge. On its watchtowers he could still see the tiny figures of the guards. The village lay in shadow while the peak directly above it glowed gold in the setting sun.

As he turned away he saw that Javaret also was looking back. He could not see her face behind its veil but he could see tears in her eyes. For a moment he wondered if she were thinking about her unfinished rug. He smiled to comfort her, but she did not look his way. Fatimat rode looking straight ahead. If she regretted leaving safety, no one would ever know.

Jemal-Edin dimly remembered leaving another village like this, the village of Gimri where he was born. They had never returned there. Gimri was leveled by Russian cannon, the stone of its buildings made rubble. For that, if for nothing else, he hated the Infidels. Gimri had been home. When they lived there, he thought, it was peaceful; Shamil was always at home or nearby studying in the mosque. But after they left Gimri and left his father behind to head the defense of the village, all had changed.

Now, no matter where they lived, his father was seldom there but gone for months at a time with the army. Now Jemal-Edin was never in a village where he felt he truly belonged, where the men of his family had always lived and owned land, where one could say "My father and my father's father and his father before him slept under this roof." Now he lived not "at home" but in other people's houses, houses lent to the Imam only for the time he needed them. To Jemal-Edin they were only places to sleep—not home. And so he left Dargo with no regret.

Hassan had ordered that they make as little noise as possible. Because the path was narrow, they rode single file. Conversation was impossible.

For three hours or more they rode ever downward from the heights on which Dargo stood. The narrow rock-ledge trail led into equally narrow canyons. Those canyons into other canyons. Then would come a ledge so narrow that it would seem only a goat could walk there.

By nightfall they had entered a vast amphitheater carved from the rock by centuries of climatic erosion, passed steles of stone capped by balancing rocks and circled eroded formations of tuffa. It was a land alien to man, a haunt of the wind and rain. They paused there to rest the horses and to eat a little of the food they carried. Jemal-Edin noticed that Javaret dismounted with difficulty. His mother assisted her to a seat on a boulder and gave her water.

The two boys walked with the warriors and led the horses to drink from a small stream rushing over the stones. The horses were allowed to drink only sparingly of the icy water.

The night wind had risen and blew across the amphitheater in gusts that sheeted off the rock walls and shuddered against the delicate formations in its bowl.

"Do you hear that?" Faizil, the warrior, asked Jemal-Edin in a harsh whisper. "Do you think it is only the wind?" In the dark the man's white face accented by his black eyebrows and thick mustache was a blur above them.

Kazi Mohammed, who had overheard the question as the warrior had intended he should, moved closer to his brother and slipped his hand under the older boy's arm for protection.

"Yes . . . only the wind," said Jemal-Edin, but without great sureness. It was a frightening sound.

"No!" Faizil shook his head. "Only sometimes is it the wind. But on other nights—nights like this when

there is no moon and blackness covers our mountains
—the sound you think and pray is the wind is much
more than that! It is the beating wings of the great
white bird, Simurg!"

Kazi Mohammed caught his breath in fright and
even Jemal-Edin shivered, but he managed to squeeze
his little brother's hand to reassure him and show him
he was not impressed with this story.

"On nights like this," said Faizil, "Simurg leaves his
foul nest and in the darkness flies across the mountains. He hunts for victims. His beak and claws are
curved and cruel as Persian blades. His eyes are huge
and glow with yellow flame. With one eye he looks
upon the past, with the other upon the future. Should
he see you—and stretch down his talons and grab you
up . . ." Faizil made his hands into grasping talons and
reached out toward Kazi Mohammed. In the darkness
the gesture lost some of its effectiveness but it was
enough to thoroughly frighten the little boy. "He car-
ries his victims to the peak high above Gimri where
all is desolation, and there he holds his awful orgies!"

"Aieyah!" Kazi Mohammed whimpered in fear.

"That is not true! That is just a story to scare babies!" Jemal-Edin declared, indignant and embarrassed because he too was frightened. "Do not be
scared, my brother. It is just a story."

"Have you ever seen Simurg?" asked Faizil.

"Nnnn-no!" shuddered Kazi Mohammed, obviously
expecting him to appear at any time.

"Have you?" demanded Jemal-Edin.

"Until you have seen him," said Faizil, ignoring the

question, "then you must believe in his existence! For if he were not real, then how could men tell stories of him?"

"Because they wish to frighten children," Hassan said from the darkness behind them, "when they should be checking the shoes of their horses to see that no nails are loose. You boys, check your mounts. I have already seen to the women's horses. We must move."

The bluntness of the man's manner was the calming effect the boys needed at that moment. They sighed with relief as if released from a spell and, gratefully, did as Hassan ordered.

"I know it was just a story . . . I think," Kazi Mohammed said as they tested the tightness of the horseshoes, "but it could be true. Couldn't it?"

"No!" said Jemal-Edin. But in his heart he hoped Faizil told no more stories like that one. The wind here did not sound natural. He was as glad as his brother when they rode out of the hollow and on down the mountain.

After midnight fatigue overtook him and he rode only half-awake, and that only to keep Kazi Mohammed from falling asleep and falling off his pony. The wind had died and the only sounds on the mountain were those of hoofsteps and the creak of saddle leather and harness. In the still night the stars overhead were many and very bright. Once he saw a light flicker on a distant mountain, then go out. There was no village in that direction. No Murid warrior would light a fire at night. Perhaps it was a shepherd's hut high on a ridge. Hassan seemingly had not seen it. Or if he had, he paid no attention to it.

There was a muffled sound from the pony ahead, and Kazi half fell out of the saddle. Fatimat pulled up and slipped down from her horse. "You lead the pony," she commanded Jemal-Edin. "I am taking him with me." She lifted the little boy down and carried him back and set him on a rug in front of her saddle, them remounted. The caravan went on.

After a time Jemal-Edin was yawning so much that his eyes teared. The rhythmic clop of hoofs, the sway of the horse, all combined to put him to sleep. When they stopped after reaching the tree line in the hour before dawn, it was all he could do to stay awake long enough to unsaddle and hobble Baba and the pony. He managed to say his prayers before rolling himself up in his rug and falling into a deep sleep. The last thought he had before he passed out was that he was glad for once that he was not yet a warrior. If he were a warrior now, he might have to stand guard.

HE WAS WAKENED BY HIS MOTHER IN MID-MORNING. "IT
is time to go," she said.

For a moment her words made no sense. In his
sleep he had forgotten where he was and was surprised to find himself outside with fir needles overhead and the sun in his eyes. Then he remembered.
"Hassan said we would travel by night," he protested.

"Javaret cannot follow the trail over the Andi
Gates. The climb would kill her. I have told Hassan
so. Now we will follow the ridge to the river and cross
over to the high plateau."

"But that is forbidden . . ."

"Shh-h-h. We have little time," she interrupted.
"There are Cossack scouts in the lower canyon. We
must be gone long before they reach this point."

Cossacks! This word drove other thoughts from his
mind. Although he had never seen one, from infancy
he had been taught to hate them. Shamil said Cos-

sacks were the dogs of their Russian masters, vicious curs guarding the boundaries of the land the Infidels stole from the mountain tribes. Stories of Cossack brutality were legend in Daghestan, a land where savagery had for centuries been refined to high art.

Jemal-Edin did not have to be told what capture by them would mean. He had seen the heads they left on pikes as warnings of what happened to captives. Leaving his mother to rouse Kazi Mohammed, he hurriedly said his prayers, rolled up his rug, and tended to nature's needs behind a nearby rock.

The men had the horses saddled and waiting, and a few minutes later the party moved out. The boys ate as they rode.

A cliff above made it impossible to gain the ridge from where they were. They traveled down the mountain to a more promising route. A few miles down the trail they rode into high spring.

Even the most weather-wizened, wind-twisted tree bore green leaves. Everywhere Jemal-Edin looked he could see waterfalls cascading down the cliffs from the melting snows high above. The falls sparkled and foamed and roared in the sunshine, where they formed pools, bright rainbows jeweled in the mist above the water. Dipping birds darted in and out of the streams, hunting, bathing, and flitting about. In every sunny space wildflowers bloomed from the carpet of pine needles. Big yellow wild roses reared high over their brambles and clustered to soften the harshness of the rocks and fill the air with their sweetness. Nutcracker birds scolded in the trees.

Where the canyon widened a small green meadow

lay hidden in a crook of the mountain. Here they surprised a herd of browsing deer, does with fawns who
bounced away on stalk-thin jerky legs. At the edge of
the meadow one fawn stopped abruptly and turned
for a last curious look at the intruders. Then, with a
just-one-more-time look on his pointy face, he dropped
to his knees and rolled in the lush grass. His mother
wheeled in her flight, circled back and gave her erring
child a chastising bite on the rump. The two boys
laughed with delight, their shrill giggles echoing from
rimrock to rimrock.

Instantly all adult eyes were on them, cold and ac-
cusing. The high-pitched sound would carry a mile in
the still air. Kazi Mohammed turned to look back at
his brother, his eyes big with guilt and fear. Jemal-
Edin gave a hopeless little shrug that said the damage
was done; they could not take back the careless
laughter.

A few minutes later they heard the crack of a musket shot. Before the echo died an answering shot
came from farther down the canyon behind them.
Now Jemal-Edin felt real fear flood him. Their laughter had been overheard by the Cossack scouts.

Hassan pulled aside and waved the others on. He
did not look at the boys as they passed him. When the
last two warriors reached him, they stopped. Looking
back, Jemal-Edin could see the three men talking.
Then Hassan took the packhorse reins. The warriors
turned and rode back in the direction from which the
shots had come.

"You will be responsible for these until the men
return," said Hassan softly as he caught up to the

boys and handed each a packhorse lead. "See that you make less noise than they do. Our lives depend on it."

Avar horses were trained to silence. They did not whicker or whinny at the scent or sound of another horse or any other animal, including man. The boys knew by Hassan's expression that he was angry with them. They also knew that had they not been their father's sons he would have severely punished them for such carelessness. But then, had they not been Shamil's sons, they would still be safe at Dargo with their mother and Javaret.

Hassan reassumed the lead and they rode faster, moving up, out of the natural trail of the canyon, heading toward its rim. It was not easy leading the packhorses. They did not care for so lowly a duty as carrying freight. They were used to the burden of a rider, accustomed to a weight that moved with them, not this lump strapped where their saddles should be. So they pulled back and twisted their heads and shied at every rolling stone and every breeze that blew. Sometimes it was all Kazi Mohammed could do to retain his seat and still keep hold of the towrope. If he tied it to the pony's harness, the packhorse simply tugged backwards and refused to move. Jemal-Edin was having only a little less trouble with his horse.

By afternoon they had left the greenery behind and were again back along the high mountain ridge. Here there was no water, only rock and strips of lingering snow. The wind blew unobstructed and even the blazing sun could not remove its chill.

From this height the riders could look down the

length of the canyonlike valley far below. Jemal-Edin strained his eyes to see Cossacks. But he saw nothing. Not even the Murid warriors he knew were down there stalking their prey.

Twice the riders had to dismount and lead the horses up and around crevasses left by winter avalanches. Freezing and the weight of heavy winter snows had broken off great sections of rock from the crest and sent it sliding down. Talus and jumbled stones marked the paths down to the tree line. Here the enormous weight and speed of the sliding debris sheered off everything in its path and left a stubble of jagged gray stumps.

The ridge grew lower, as if the mountains were preparing to greet the river which bisected them not far ahead. The peaks to the west had cut off the sun. The party rode in shade, zigzagging downward, Hassan leading them where the horses could find footing on the smooth flow rock. The slope was so steep that Fatimat and Faizil rode flanking Javaret who was now so exhausted that it was all she could do to cling to the saddle. While Fatimat guided the other woman's horse, Faizil kept a firm grip on Javaret's arm to keep her from falling forward.

Jemal-Edin dismounted. Giving Baba's reins to Kazi Mohammed, he led the packhorses down himself. His little brother was too tired to protest this special treatment. After an hour or more of downward travel, Hassan brought them to a halt. They had reached the bridge.

It was a natural bridge of stone spanning a canyon cut by patient water over eons of time. On both sides of the canyon crenelated cliffs brushed with green pines led treacherously down to the shining river far below. Air drafts rose from the canyon as the water vapor cooled, boiled up, and flowed over the rim, bringing the scents of pine and clean wet stone. The horses shifted restlessly. They, too, were tired and thirsty and longed to rest.

Fifteen feet wide at its narrowest point and twice that thick at its arch, the bridge was more than sturdy enough to support any load that could reach it on these heights. But still it looked frail and perilous, as if any century now it too would be crushed by the weight of time and tumble down for eternity.

Hassan rode forward alone to make sure no outrider waited to waylay them. As he crossed the bridge his horse shied a little and did a sideways dance that made Jemal-Edin thrust his hand in his mouth to keep from crying out. But horse and rider reached the other bank safely and turned and came back.

"We will cover the eyes of the pack animals," Hassan said as he rode up to the boys. "Without a rider they might panic." He tied a black cloth over the eyes of one while Jemal-Edin did the other. "We must cross the bridge quickly. While on it we can be seen for miles up and down the river. You, most noble Fatimat, will go first since it is your safety that most concerns the Imam. Aziz and Faizil will take the second wife and her horse across. Then the Imam's sons. I will follow with the pack animals."

"I will walk across and lead Baba," said Jemal-Edin.

"No," said Hassan. "You must ride. Never let your

horse feel you are afraid." He waited until Jemal-Edin had remounted. The warriors had returned from taking Javaret's horse across and now took Kazi Mohammed. Jemal-Edin was to follow by himself.

Like Jemal-Edin, Baba was not sure he liked the bridge. He felt safe on the heights; the narrowest goat path never fazed him so long as he could keep one eye looking at a solid rock wall. But to carry his rider out over three hundred feet of openness, with a silver ribbon of river far below made him skittish. It made Jemal-Edin a little sick to his stomach to look down. Both horse and boy breathed a sigh of relief when they reached the other side. Then Hassan crossed.

"Come," he told the others as he rode past them. "We must be far from this place before we sleep."

He led them down through the barren landscape of stone toward the pines visible far below. The mountains were still so high that the valleys were night-filled although it was more than two hours before sunset. In the scrub several thousand feet below, a brown bear, out for his evening meal, caught the scent of horse on the wind and reared up on his hind legs to sniff the air more carefully. With his near-sighted eyes he could not see them, but he knew they were up there in the direction in which he was peering. Jemal-Edin saw him standing like a sentinel, seemingly watching them pass.

Far up on a peak there was a flash of white as a herd of mountain goats leaped from one crag to another. As he watched them the boy wondered if what his father had told him were true, that goats liked to lie and watch the sunset, taking an almost human joy in its beauty.

They spent the night in an abandoned shepherd's hut on the edge of a high plateau. In a less dangerous spring, this plateau, an alpine meadowland so vast it took a rider half a day to cross it, would have been pastureland for sheep and goats. But this spring the huts hidden among the rocky ridges lining the meadow were deserted, and the uncropped grass grew high and lush with wildflowers.

The huts were built of stone and so cunningly concealed amid the rocks that a rider could gallop over their rock-slab roofs without realizing he had just ridden over a human dwelling. To enter one was like walking into an animal's burrow. As he followed his mother inside, Jemal-Edin felt the hair rise on his arms.

But Fatimat seemed almost at home here. Telling him to wait in the entry tunnel with the others, she entered alone, and he heard her moving around in the darkness. After a moment there was a spark, then a small flame lit up the inner room. With the aid of the tinderbox and flint carried always in her coat, Fatimat had lit a fire. It was safe to do so here; the walls shielded the light and the night hid the smoke.

Before her sons had time to sit down and realize how tired they were from the thin air, she sent them for the rugs and food from the packs so that she might make Javaret comfortable, and feed them all before they slept.

Outside, the horses, freed of their riders for the first

time in many hours, were rolling in the long grass. They were watched over carefully by the warriors to see that the hungry animals did not overeat and so give themselves a painful case of bloat. Jemal-Edin untied the packs. Taking out the flat cooking pan, the bag of rice and packs of food wrapped in oiled leather, he handed them to Kazi Mohammed who stood beside him, barely awake.

"Take these in to Mother. I will bring the bedding."

Kazi stumbled off in the direction of the hut, gave the articles to his mother, and then dropped to the floor beside Javaret. She put her arm around him and the two leaned together for support.

"Tell the Naib Hassan that if he will be good enough to have one of the men bring us water, I will prepare pilaf for us all," Fatimat said when Jemal-Edin returned.

He looked at her kneeling before the crude fireplace, its flames reflected in her eyes and shining off her black hair. Although he did not know it then, it was a scene he would remember always until, as he grew older, it haunted him. His mother in her flowered silk trousers and coat, her white facial veil loose and hanging like a soft scarf around her throat, her intelligent eyes circled with fatigue, her slender elegant hands black with grime from feeding the fire. She was a noblewoman; she was his mother—and this . . . this should not be! For a reason he did not understand then, he felt tears burning his eyes and impulsively he threw his arms around her neck and hugged her.

"What is it, my son?" she asked, putting her arms

about him. And when he could not tell her, instead of saying "Are you afraid?" she said, "We are safe here. We are all tired now. But we are safe—and in a little time we will feel better, when we have hot food inside us." She brushed his hair away from his face, held him away from her and smiled into his eyes. "Between the two of us, we can take care of our sleepy family. If you can get us some water . . . ?"

Half embarrassed by his emotion, he brushed the tears from his eyes and smiled back at her, then planting a sloppy kiss on her forehead, he turned and ran out to do the errand. Had she asked him then to kill the bear he had seen earlier that evening, he would have attempted to do it for her.

THEY LEFT AT DAWN THE NEXT MORNING. EVEN THEN, as they saddled the horses, Jemal-Edin heard Hassan grumbling to the warriors about being delayed by women and children. Jemal-Edin did not appreciate that remark. He did not consider himself a "child" and his mother had been the first one up.

While Hassan was always correct in his behavior toward the Imam's family, Jemal-Edin did not much like him. He sensed that where he and his mother were concerned, the feeling was mutual. Hassan was the Imam's most trusted aide and would remain so— until Jemal-Edin grew old enough to replace him.

Hot food and a good night's sleep had done much to restore the strength and spirits of Kazi Mohammed. He was bubbling to himself, running about the dew-soaked meadow trying to catch small grass frogs that somehow managed to live through the cold nights. When he mounted up he had to put three frogs into his lambskin hat so that his hands would be free for the reins and the packhorse lead. Even Javaret smiled at this. It was obvious that she, too, felt better.

Today's ride promised to be much easier. Half of it they would spend on this plateau, the other half making their way down almost to the lowlands to reach the final portion of their trail. By tomorrow evening, Allah willing, they would be riding up the switchbacks to Akhulgo's peak.

At midmorning Jemal-Edin, who was riding last in line, heard faint hoofbeats. He saw Hassan half rise in his saddle and look back. They were in the open; there was no place to hide. All of them, warriors, women, and children, drew their rifles and waited. Two horsemen came galloping over the crest behind them. As they sighted the caravan, they waved. It was the two warriors who had set out to find the Cossacks. They galloped past, their faces streaked with dust. After talking with them for a short time, Hassan gave them a wave of dismissal and rode on, leaving them to wait until the packhorses passed. They took over the pack leads as if they had only been gone a moment, saying nothing to the two boys.

But Jemal-Edin noticed that each carried a grisly trophy of their night's work. Beside the saddle of each, strung on a leather thong, flopped a collection of right hands removed from the Cossack outriders— who had probably died in their sleep, their throats slit. This taking of hands was a custom among some of the tribes. A custom Shamil disapproved of, but would do nothing to discourage until the Infidels had been driven from Daghestan. As Jemal-Edin looked at the battle trophies in revolted fascination, he found his stomach growing queasy.

Fatimat, too, had noticed them as the warriors passed by. She turned to see her first-born staring at them, his face pale. Kicking her horse into a run, she caught up with Hassan and spoke to him, then returned to her place in line. After a few minutes, to show that he was not accustomed to being ordered about by women, even noblewomen, Hassan rode back along the line.

"The wife of the Imam humbly asks that you do not display those," he said, not looking at the men but pointing to the hands. "As you know, the Imam's second wife is in a delicate condition. The first wife believes the sight of these will cause the woman illness."

No Murid ever questioned the request or command of an officer. To do so meant instant death. "May we keep them?" one asked, "if we cover them?"

"No. Leave them for the vultures. Your bravery is well known. I shall tell the Imam of your feat."

Without waiting to see them dropped into the high grass he rode off.

"What was that all about?" Kazi Mohammed wanted to know. Jemal-Edin told him.

"Aw . . . I didn't get to see them!" The little boy was disappointed. "You did not tell me . . . where are they now?"

"Back there—and do not ride back!"

"But I want to . . ."

"No you don't. You just think you do."

The edge of the plateau was rimmed by a pine forest that led down the mountainside. The trail here was good. It had been used by generations of shepherds driving their flocks to summer pasture. Although the party stopped twice for brief rest periods, they made good time. The pines faded into hardwoods—oak, sycamore, beech, and elm.

Jemal-Edin rode along daydreaming of times to come when he would ride as his father's lieutenant. There was nothing else to do. Even chatterbox Kazi had run out of things to talk about. Off in the woods warblers trilled, a thrush burbled its liquid song, and other thrushes answered like echoes. Squirrels chattered at the horses, questioning their right to be there. The clear air smelled of horse and leather, pine, leaf mold, and ferns.

The ride assumed the monotony of familiarity—descend one slope, ride along a canyon, ascend up out of the canyon along the ridge of the next mountain. After midday from somewhere to the north came the distant booms of sporadic cannon fire. It, too, was a familiar sound to Jemal-Edin. It had echoed through these mountains since his birth and for thirty years before that. The adults might talk about it, speculating over which village was being shelled, which friend or relative was in danger of death; but to the boy it was as natural as the thunder it resembled.

A few clouds of fog began drifting over, shrouding the peaks. The wind whipped up and heavier clouds were driven in from the east. Where all had been sunshine, now black gloom hung overhead. The horses began to shy at every rolling pebble, every dry weedstalk the wind brushed against their slender ankles.

When Jemal-Edin reached back and pulled his hooded leather cloak from his saddle roll, Baba shied, snorted and trembled as if his rider were about to set devils on him. The boy soothed the nervous horse as best he could, but it was plain that Baba was not going to be thoroughly comforted until the storm was over.

They were riding a gentle slope left by a glacier long since melted. In the pockets of rich soil the ice floe left behind, trees had taken root and grown tall and old. It was a pleasant place to ride any time but during an electrical storm. None in the party needed Hassan to tell them to keep away from the trees. All the mountain people knew it was not the roar of the thunder that counted but the crackling white fury of the lightning. As the wind blew the storm clouds ever closer, the little caravan snaked its way along avoiding the trees—vulnerable beneath the open sky.

Then suddenly the threatening clouds were overhead and it seemed as if the lightning was aiming for them. Without warning a fusillade of bolts tore into the ground to their right like some evil giant's plow, flinging earth, sand, and stone fragments in a vicious hail. The terrified horses screamed and reared and tried to bolt, and each rider instantly became too busy saving his seat to think about anyone else.

Baba, born wild on the plains of Astrakhan, had known storms like this since he was a colt. He did what all wild things do in face of danger. He ran as fast as he could! There was nothing Jemal-Edin could do but hold on. A sharp fragment of lightning-split stone flew through the air cutting the boy's cheek. He never felt the pain. In a few seconds he had passed all the riders but one. There ahead of Baba, but running faster, was Javaret's normally placid brown mare. The young woman was leaning forward, her arms wrapped about the saddle pommel, holding on for her life. The mare was running for shelter, directly toward a tall stand of pines.

The thunder that followed the lightning cracked and rolled overhead. Baba veered sideways and put on more speed. The initial fright faded, and Jemal-Edin began to think again as he watched the blurred ground below fly past. Javaret's horse must not gain the trees. To do so right now was to invite death. He hunched down like a jockey and fought to gain command of Baba's wild run.

Behind him he could hear his mother's voice and Faizil's shouting. He could not hear what they said. Ahead he saw Javaret's arm reach down, trying to grab the reins she had dropped when her mare bolted. But her swollen body was in the way.

There was no point in using the whip. Baba could run no faster. In fact, Jemal-Edin had never known the horse could run this fast. Ahead, the mare, burdened with twice the weight Baba carried, began to slow, but she was still running well.

"Ayp! Ayp! Ayp!" the boy yipped in Baba's ears. This was the signal he used when he and Baba raced with the other boys. Baba's ears pricked up—perhaps he could be fooled into thinking this was a race. As they began to gain, the mare looked back and saw the other horse running behind. To her that meant there was still danger and she put on a burst of new speed.

The two horses were within twenty yards of the pines when Jemal-Edin managed to reach over and grab the mare's reins. With both hands he tugged them over and wrapped them around the high pommel of his saddle, at the same time guiding Baba to the left with his knees. He saw Javaret's veil had blown away and her hair had shaken free of the scarfs wrapped around her head. Her face was very young and very pale but she was all right. It took more than a runaway horse to scare a mountain woman.

"Thank you, little brother," she said when the horses had slowed to a trot. "I never knew I was riding the mother of champions or I would have been more prepared for such speed. Did you know she could run like this?"

"No," said Jemal-Edin, shaking his head as he gave the reins over to her, "I don't think anyone did. Are you all right?"

She nodded yes. "But we must find low ground." She turned rather awkwardly in her saddle to look back. "I do not see the others."

"All the horses bolted," said Jemal-Edin. "But yours and mine bolted in the same direction."

"We will find them after the storm," Javaret said calmly.

But if she was truly calm, or trying to be, the horses still were not. Lightning and thunder were cracking all around. One tree was struck to the heart and splintered by the explosion that sent pieces flying so hard they pronged upright into the ground and quivered there. The air was thick with the smell of ozone and the clouds overhead were heavy with rain. On the other side of a rise they saw a wide shallow creek. Just ahead was a drop and they turned aside to gallop down a ramplike dike of stone toward the water.

"There!" Javaret called and pointed off to the left. Its base scoured away, the small cliff above jutted out to form a deep roof and a space big enough not only for them but for the horses. As they turned toward it they could see the rain coming toward them like a curtain. They had no more than gained shelter before the downpour began.

Once dismounted they were only a little less grateful than their horses to be in out of the storm. They walked the animals back to where the cliff ended in a three-sided cave. Here, it was plain from the old horse manure on the rock floor, previous travelers had taken refuge. The rain came down with such a roar it almost muted the thunder.

Javaret made her way back rather painfully over the jumble of boulders and windswept debris to sit down on a stone and lean against the rock wall and close her eyes. Jemal-Edin stayed beside the horses, staring out at the white curtain of rain and hail.

After five minutes or so he was glad to see the rest of the party emerge from the downpour, come galloping up, and one by one duck under the ledge. Their hands were cut by hailstones and bleeding, but none had fallen victim to the lightning, and their wide leather cloaks had kept them fairly dry.

An hour later the sky was as clear as if there had been no storm.

THE TREES GREW MORE SCARCE. MANY OF THE PINES
looked diseased. The leaves of the hardwoods were
sickly and wizened. There was a strange smell in the
air, harsh and unpleasant. To breathe it for a few
minutes blotted out all other odors. The horses
snorted and sneezed repeatedly, trying to clear their
nostrils. The humans fastened scarfs across their
faces.

Then there were no more trees. The land was de-
void of any green, the earth was bare sand and clay,
littered with rock slabs flung about as if by angry
giants. The trail picked its way among strange glisten-
ing mounds whose surface cut a thousand tiny
wounds when touched. It circled pools not of water
but of some noxious tarry liquid that stank in the sun.
Scattered along the shores and half submerged in the
pools were the oil-soaked decaying corpses of birds

and animals who had made the fatal mistake either of drinking or of trying to swim here.

It had been cool on the mountains. It was warm here. An airless uncomfortable warmth as though even the wind feared this place. This desolation was known and feared throughout the mountains as a place of evil. The old men had spoken truly, Jemal-Edin thought. It was the landscape of a nightmare!

Here on this petroleum-soaked plateau northeast of Gimri, all the creatures of Daghestani tribal superstition had their ancient home. The legends and myths of imperial Persia had seeped into the mountain fastnesses centuries before. Trapped here in the cultural backwater, they had mutated. Like any story told from one culture to the next, from one generation to the next, these legends altered from Persian to Daghestani, from tribe to tribe, from sect to sect.

The Persian's giant firebird embodying goodness and knowledge became the horrible Simurg. The thirty smaller firebirds were corrupted into various monsters of mountain myth. When impure souls barred from Paradise fell back to earth to fulfill their penance, they fell here. In these mountains they became not the peri, a creature of earthly delight, but spirits more evil than any human could imagine. Here the amiable genie-of-the-lamp became the wicked djinn who did everything from laming a horse to causing plagues.

And although belief in the Koran and in its prophet, Mohammed, had been the official religion of Daghestan since the ninth century, still these superstitions persisted—though now people disclaimed them as tales told to children. But still no tribesman would venture onto this plateau after dark, and only dire necessity would force them to cross it in daylight.

Because of this Jemal-Edin was surprised to see the trail they rode was an old one and very heavily traveled.

"The devs and imps use it!" Faizil told him when he asked. Kazi Mohammed gave his pony a swat and closed the space between himself and his mother's horse. "The devs and imps have cloven feet like goats and horns, too, and eyes that . . ."

"But the trail was made by horses," said Jemal-Edin, familiar by now with Faizil's teasing. "Not goats. By horses carrying heavy loads."

"Undoubtedly they were ridden by giants," Faizil assured him solemnly.

The boy grinned at him. "No, Faizil, truly? Who comes here?"

"Tribesmen," admitted the man.

"Why?"

"I cannot say."

"Why not?"

"The Imam forbids it."

Jemal-Edin frowned. Faizil was obviously not going to tell him anything. He would ask his mother when there was a chance of speaking with her alone.

They camped in a small ravine in a spot above the plain where the wind blew from behind them, carrying the scent away. There was grass here but the horses would not eat it. Nor would they touch the leaves. All were covered by a fine black soot. The water in the nearby spring was iridescent with oil but that in the small waterfalls coming from high up the ridge was pure. Jemal-Edin was nearly asleep when he heard from far in the distance the sound of men chanting.

He looked over to see if his brother had heard it, his ears being even sharper. But Kazi was asleep, as apparently was everyone else except Faizil who stood the first guard tonight. Jemal-Edin could see the man's silhouette against the night sky; he was seated motionless upon the rocks like a gargoyle, his cloak open and flaring like black wings folded behind him.

Silently Jemal-Edin slid out of his covers, and crawled on his belly away from the other sleepers. Young as he was, he made no noise. No stone crunched beneath his weight to betray him. No dried weed crackled. He had been well taught in the art of guerrilla warfare. Had he needed to, he could have crept up on the watchman and dispatched him with his dagger.

But thoughts like that were far from his mind at the moment. All he wanted to do now was to find out who was chanting. And why? It did not sound like a Murid chant, but who else could be this deep into his father's territory?

When he was far enough away from Faizil for the wind to cover any slight noise he might make, he pushed himself cautiously to his feet and hurried back down the trail toward the flatland. When free of the rock formations he saw to his great surprise, and not a little fear, that there were low fires all across the plain. Not campfires, but curious flames of blue and orange and yellow that jetted and danced in the wind.

For many minutes he stood there, his heart beating loudly in his ears, watching the sight and wondering, remembering every scary story he had ever been told of this place and thinking they were all probably true. There was a small flurry of stones to his right and he jumped, expecting a demon to fling itself on him. Instead he saw the dim form of a fox slinking away in the darkness. The sight reassured him; wild creatures did not hunt where there was danger.

From here it seemed that the chanting was coming from a point to the east where the fires burned brightest. He headed that way and soon found himself on a well-traveled path. They had merely circled the outskirts of the deadland this afternoon, he saw as he walked. This new trail led into its depths.

After half a mile or more the land sloped down, the depth of the depression hidden by jumbled piles of stone. Jemal-Edin left the trail and made his way up to the top of the nearest stone pile and stretched flat upon a slab.

Below in the hollow was a perfect circle of fire. It burned from a liquid; he could see the flames flickering over its shiny black surface. Around the circle of flames whirled seven men, naked except for their white turbans and a swath of white cloth about their middles. As they whirled in their dance they chanted, their voices high-pitched in the ecstasy of hysterical supplication.

Dervishes!

He had seen them before, gaunt, hollow-eyed hermits who sometimes wandered into the village begging for shelter and food. When they appeared many of the women would spit and turn away and make the sign that protected them from the evil eye. His father, Shamil, did not fully approve of the sects although he gave word that none were to be harmed. It was not that they were Infidels, but that the god they worshipped was not Shamil's god but an older, more mysterious force. Some said it was the sun; some said it was the universe, and some said All Was One in Allah. Whatever their faith, Shamil believed it too vague and too complicated for a good Murid to understand. He gave them traditional hospitality but almost never allowed them to dance.

Now, below, one of the men fell to the ground in a stupor or trance. The others paid him no heed but went on, their voices becoming louder and more shrill. The man on the ground began to twitch and writhe in what looked like the agony of convulsions, his eyes rolling far back in his head so that only the whites showed in the firelight. Jemal-Edin watched in fascination as the dance became faster.

With no warning a rope slid around the boy's neck and was jerked tight! He gave a little yelp of fear and rolled sideways, straight up against the feet of his captor, an old man in sandals. Dressed in a long and very filthy white djellaba, the bearded wild-haired old man towered above him, clutching in his gnarled hands the other end of the rope.

Jemal-Edin was so surprised by his presence, and by the fact that the old man had been able to creep up on him, that for a moment he could think of nothing but the question "Who are you? What are you doing?" He spoke in Avar. The old man did not answer so he repeated the question in Arabic.

At this the old man gave the rope a quick jerk, turned and with surprising nimbleness made his way off the rocks, forcing Jemal-Edin to follow to avoid being choked. As he walked along he tried to loosen the noose. Each time he got it partially free, the old man jerked him nearly off his feet. Finally, in irritation, Jemal-Edin pulled his dagger and cut the rope.

"You will displease Him! You will be punished!" The voice was deep and strong. Jemal-Edin backed away as the old man wheeled about to accuse him, but he kept the knife unsheathed and pointed at this possible enemy.

"He sent you to me as a reward for my prayers. You are to be my slave, my son, my servant to care for me in my old age! You are my reward for devotion! Why else would you be here—a child alone in this sacred and terrible place? No child comes here!"

"I am no one's slave!" said Jemal-Edin, "I am the first-born son of the Imam Shamil!"

"You are a beggar orphan, an outcast. You have been sent to serve me!"

"No," said Jemal-Edin shaking his head and thinking the old man must have been driven mad by loneliness. "Who are you, old man? What are you doing here? Are you a hermit dervish? Are you like those down there?"

"You blaspheme!" The old man at first seemed very angry, but then, as he thought about it, he said. "It is only right that you should not recognize a man who no longer has the need for a name." He shook his head as if Jemal-Edin's ignorance of him was a confirmation of something he had suspected. He stared past the boy and beyond, no longer seeing him.

"I see with the eyes of Allah, hear with the ears of Allah, speak with the tongue of Allah and work with the hands of Allah. I have truly followed the Path to Him and become One with Him. I am one of the poles on which the earth turns," he assured the dim stars overhead.

Jemal-Edin did not believe that the earth turned, and he was not impressed with the old man's claims to holiness. He stood looking up at him, still defiantly clutching his dagger in readiness, rubbing his chaffed neck with the other hand.

"You doubt me, you son of an imp!" the old man said, then added grimly, "I shall show you my power! Come!"

He stalked off into the dark shadows cast by the rocks, his robe ghostly in the flickering light. After hesitating a moment, Jemal-Edin followed at a cautious distance. He had nearly been captured once. Perhaps there were other madmen hiding here? The old man came to an opening in a cairn of rocks and disappeared into the cave mouth. He reappeared almost at once, a bow and quiver of arrows in his hands.

"Stay here," he ordered. "I shall awaken the fire-birds and by my will hold them at bay. Then you shall believe me. Then you shall serve me!"

In spite of himself, the boy shivered. The old man circled around the hollow, keeping out of sight of the still-chanting dervishes, and disappeared behind some boulders. After straining his eyes trying to catch another glimpse of him, Jemal-Edin turned his attention to the cave where the hermit apparently lived. He stuck his head in the entrance but it was too dark to see anything. The place smelled as stale as a wolf's den.

Minutes passed and the boy began to worry. What if someone at camp missed him and came hunting for him? They would not be pleased. And if they told his father . . . He fidgeted, wanting to go but half afraid to disobey the command of the madman.

Then a flash caught his eye. Someone was shooting arrows dipped in pitch. The first arrow arched up like a meteor, then its light blurred and spread as it entered the layer of smoke and haze over the land before sinking from sight. A second arrow followed, then a third and fourth.

From the direction where the first arrow fell to earth came a poof! and then a low rumble. Then, roaring high into the air came a jet of flame.

For a moment it was the purest blue tipped with gold, a thing so beautiful he sucked in his breath with a hiss of awe. But it spread and lost form, the blue faded to orange, and it pulsated in the wind and hissed like a thousand serpents. To its right another flame sprang up, pure blue like the first before it too became corrupted.

From the hollow below a great cry went up, and he saw all the men fall to their knees and cower before the fires hovering above them. It took him a moment before he realized they were praying to the flames.

There was another roar and then an explosion that

made the earth tremble beneath his feet. A third flame shot up, this one dwarfing all the others. The earth continued to rumble and shake.

He, too, wanted to fall onto his knees, but his fear was so great that he could only stand as if rooted to the unsteady ground and watch the great flame torching against the darkness. There came a smell now of something old and decayed, a bitterness that choked in his throat and made his eyes tear. As the wind fed the flames and they danced against its thrust, it seemed to him that it was indeed a giant bird— Simurg flexing his wings of fire! If it managed to rise free from the earth, it would be too late for him!

He turned and, with a cry of terror choking in his throat, began to run as if all the evil spirits in the place were chasing him. It was easy to find the trail. In the light from the flames the hoofprints were a pattern of shine and shadow on the sand.

In his fright he missed the turnoff Hassan had taken to the camp. He had gone a quarter of a mile past it before he realized his mistake and turned back. Only when his sides hurt so badly from running that he had to squeeze them with both arms did he slow down. By that time he was halfway back to camp and the light of the fires was far in the distance.

The farther he got from the flames, the more calmly he could think about them. It slowly occurred to him that the old man had ignited something, deliberately, with his pitch-soaked arrows. It had not been anything supernatural after all. Not firebird or monster. Dangerous, perhaps, but then all fires were dangerous. And he found he was a little disappointed.

There was the call of a nightbird where no nightbird should be, in the shadows of clay banks to his left along the trail. He stopped short and then blended into the darkness beside a rock.

"If you were my enemy, you would already be in Paradise," Faizil whispered from the darkness behind him. "You come along the path panting and huffing like a pregnant cow. Some warrior you will make."

Jemal-Edin breathed a sigh of relief. "I will be a better warrior than you are a watchman," he whispered, and Faizil appeared beside him, his smile visible by the faint gleam of his teeth.

"Very well. If you do not tell the Naib Hassan that I let you go . . . I will not tell him—or your father— that you went. Agreed?"

"Agreed," Jemal-Edin said gratefully.

"And did you satisfy your curiosity? Did you see the fire worshippers?"

"Yes. And an old hermit who did something to make the flames flare up."

"Ahh . . ." Faizil breathed. "So you found him there. You must be wary of him. It is said he is the last of the Magi. Some say he is very holy . . ." The warrior shrugged.

"Is he?"

"Holy? Or mad? How does a simple warrior tell the difference?"

"Why do the tribesmen go there?" asked the boy. "To see the hermit?"

"No. Promise you will not tell?"

Jemal-Edin promised.

"They go to get the water that burns . . . the Persians call it naphtha. If the Infidel try to scale the walls of Akhulgo, you will see how it is used in war."

Jemal-Edin absorbed this information silently. They passed the place where the horses were tethered and then he was back, safe beside his bedroll. As he stretched out on his rug he felt his mother's hand on his arm, and started with guilt. She was awake! He waited in silence for her to speak, expecting a scolding. But instead she asked, "Did you see the blue flames?"

"Yes, my mother."

"They are beautiful," she observed simply. "My father took me there once. Long ago." In the darkness her whisper was wistful, like the voice of a child. "Long ago," she repeated. Then she gave his arm a little squeeze and said, "I am glad you saw them. We must sleep now."

After he had snuggled down inside his covers again and lay looking up at the stars and watching the misty smoke drift past on the wind, he heard again the distant chanting of the fire worshippers. He fell asleep wondering what it was they prayed for. And to Whom.

The party forded the river the next day at noon and rode up the zigzag trail to Akhulgo three hours later. Shamil did not come out to meet them after their long journey. That would not have been seemly. Instead he remained closeted in counsel with his Naibs, and left his servants to settle his family into the house by the mosque which had been prepared for them.

When late that night Jemal-Edin was awakened by the angry wails of an infant, he was told Javaret had given birth to a son. Shamil had named the baby Said.

FROM WHERE HE SAT ALONE, HALF-HIDDEN BY THE walls of the watchtower roof, Jemal-Edin could see for miles across the mountains. Baba was somewhere below, in a cloud-obscured canyon that twisted back into the hills. His father had ordered all the horses hidden except those few needed by the messengers who galloped in and out of the village more frantically each day.

He was remembering that Shamil had given him Baba when he was three, and Baba, little more than a colt. The boy loved the shaggy black animal more than anything else in the world. Now he worried for its safety. What if the Russians found the horses? Would they take Baba as a pack animal? He was too small to carry heavy loads, and too small for a man to ride. Perhaps they would shoot him? He tried to imagine Baba dead, and at the thought of it tears filled his eyes and slipped down his cheeks.

"Why do you weep?"

Startled by his father's voice, Jemal-Edin jumped and his face flushed with embarrassment. Hurriedly he rubbed the offending tears away and pretended to be interested in an eagle circling over the river below. He wished his father made more noise when he walked; he was always there when you did not expect him.

"Look at me, son," commanded Shamil. "Why do you weep?"

The man towered over the boy, face impassive, waiting. Fine-boned, elegantly slender in his black clothes, Shamil's great height was accented by the crownlike lambskin hat topped by his Imam's turban. Across the chest of his close-fitting coat gleamed a double row of silver cartridge cases. His belt hugged the tooled thirty-one-inch double-edged dagger he was never without. At his right side, for he was left-handed, swung a silver-hilted saber.

Jemal-Edin looked up to see if his father were angry with him. The hooded hazel eyes were not narrowed, just watchful. That was a good sign. "I was thinking about Baba. Do you think they will hurt him, Father?"

"You weep for a pony?" The quiet disdain in Shamil's voice cut like a lash, and Jemal-Edin shrank back against the wall. "You are an Avar! The descendant of ten generations of Avar nobles! No Avar —man, woman, or child—ever weeps! Tears are a weakness! From the cradle an Avar is strong! Do you understand?"

"Yes, sir."

"If you have cause for grief, you avenge the cause with your dagger. You do not weep about it! Do you understand?"

"Yes, sir."

The man's voice softened, and he reached out and gently put his hand on his son's hair. "Our horses will be safer in the canyon than they would be up here. They have grass and water. No Russian cannon will find them there. And if the Infidel soldiers should come near him, don't you think Baba will run away from their horrible smell?"

For the first time the boy smiled and nodded. "He can run very fast, Father," he agreed, eager to believe that.

"You have done your best to protect him," Shamil assured the boy. "Now he, with the help of Allah, must protect himself. As must we all. Come with me. Come away from this place you have chosen to brood in. Before the muezzin calls for evening prayers I must make a final inspection of our defenses. I want you with me. Some of my warriors have never seen the first-born son of their Imam. I want them all to know you are here. To know my Faith is great enough to keep my most precious possession with me—here in Akhulgo."

Surprised by this unexpected tribute to himself, the boy glowed with pleasure while Shamil let the silence embroider his compliment.

The Imam looked down from the rooftop on the activity in the narrow streets below. There black-garbed Murid warriors stalked among veiled women. Children played in the narrow shafts of sunlight streaming between nearby peaks. Dogs lay sleeping. In the dusty square in front of the mosque a shiny-tailed rooster clucked with self-importance to his harem of scrawny hens.

"Also, I want you to see what I have done here," Shamil spoke again. "Someday, if Allah wills it, you will take my place. When that day comes, I want it said that not only does the father still live in his son, but that he has grown wiser. Come."

He led the way to the rough wooden ladder. When they reached the ground four of Shamil's Naibs, his most trusted officers, were waiting for him. The Imam went nowhere outside his home without bodyguards. Before these men Shamil spoke to Jemal-Edin as he would to a man. And by the custom of the Avar, in four years Jemal-Edin would be considered a man and a warrior. As they walked through the narrow streets the people gave the Imam and his son the bow of respect and submission to his authority, which Shamil with great dignity pretended to ignore. But had he not received this respect, he was capable of pulling his dagger and instantly killing the man who so insulted him.

"I have almost four thousand of my best warriors here now," he told Jemal-Edin as they walked. "For months the army of the sultan of Russia has been burning our villages, slaughtering our people and our flocks. Each time we sign a treaty of cease-fire, they break it! It must stop! We will not become the slaves of the White Sultan! You must always remember, my son, that the Russian soldiers are not like our warriors. In a small saddle pack our men can carry all they need to sustain them for weeks. But the Infidel Russians have greedy bellies. Just to feed them their army must drag huge supply wagons through the mountains. They bring along their servants, their silver, their furniture. Accordingly," and his eyes gleamed, "I have led them farther and farther from their supply camps. To reach Akhulgo they must cross miles of mountains where no road has ever been. Cross a dozen streams and rivers no bridge has ever crossed. And when they get here—we will cut them off—and then . . ." He made a violent slashing gesture with his hand that vividly indicated the fate he had in mind for the Russian army.

The small party of men had left the village now, passed through the gate and stood several hundred yards down the stony path.

"When you rode in with my wives two days ago, what did you see?" Shamil asked his son.

Jemal-Edin frowned. He had seen only a village much like the one of Dargo where he lived with his mother while his father led the resistance. Try hard as he could to think of anything unusual, he could not. And so he said honestly, "I saw . . . the village, Father." And then thinking his father wanted something more, added, "It seemed larger but quieter than ours . . ."

"You saw nothing else?"

". . . No."

"What do you see now?" Shamil swept his hand to indicate the view. "Look closely!"

Akhulgo was a fortress built atop a six-hundred-foot crag. It was surrounded on three sides by a river filled with sharp rapids. The only approach to the

crag was a narrow path, a series of natural switchbacks formed by rock outcroppings. The path could
easily be blocked and defended by a handful of men.

Jemal-Edin squinted his eyes and scanned the peak
looming above him. The walls and watchtower were
clearly visible, the houses huddled against the stone,
the minaret of the mosque, the people on the streets.
In the quiet air their voices floated down to him, the
words unintelligible. Then below the walls on the dry
terraces where the sheep and goats grazed he noticed
something. It looked like small black windows cut
into the rock. But were they there before?

"There are holes in the mountain . . . but . . . ?"

"The son of Shamil has sharp eyes," commented
one of the Naibs.

Jemal-Edin looked up at his father to see if he had
the man's approval. For an instant Shamil's hooded
eyes gleamed and then went back to their customary
stillness.

"Come," he said and strode off, the skirt of his black
coat flaring in the breeze he created. At the edge of
the lowest terrace he left the path and led Jemal-Edin
across the rocks. The boy saw that rough steps had
been cut into the rock. They led down a trench so
deep he could not see over the top.

"These trenches and the other fortifications here
were blasted out of the living rock by deserters from
the Russian army," said Shamil. "I paid them well for
their services. Of course, when they had finished
working for me, I had them put into the prison pits. A
man who deserts one army is capable of betraying
another."

Tunnels cut through the rock led under the wall to

more trenches and breastworks, then more tunnels. Jemal-Edin followed his father down the dim passages, lit only by occasional slits channeled up to the surface. The boy marveled at the size of the tunnels and, to him, their great length.

The men's soft boots made little noise on the stone floor. When they entered the first hidden blockhouse that overlooked the path down the mountain, the four sentries whirled in surprise and to a man drew their sabers. All were apologetic when they saw who their visitors were.

Shamil dismissed their words with a wave of his hand, then easily hoisted Jemal-Edin to the narrow slit opening. "From here we can fire down on the enemy with no danger. These are the holes you saw in the mountain. Four men with rifles in here can withstand a regiment trying to storm the gate. The White Sultan makes his soldiers use muskets. But then he has many men to waste. I do not." He set the boy on his feet again. "Come."

Jemal-Edin was shown the underground stables and barracks full of Murid warriors. There were even living quarters below ground for the women and children. The two springs on the peak had been roofed with rock slabs. A deep cistern had been blasted out and filled with fresh water. There were granaries filled with rice and millet and barley, jar upon jar of yogurt, cheeses, flour, herbs—all the supplies needed to sustain the population and army for a siege of months, if need be. The ammunition storehouses were large and well stocked.

"The Russian generals will see just what you saw of

Akhulgo," Shamil told his son, "another helpless village waiting to be sacked." He smiled to himself, "But then the life of a soldier tends to be boring. It might be pleasant for them to have some surprises."

As Shamil's small party came up the steps from the main ammunition storehouse, they heard a shout from the watchtower. A few moments later a messenger came galloping up the steep street. He swung down off his horse, his handsome face gray with dust and fatigue, and was met by Hassan, Shamil's First Naib. After a whispered conference Hassan returned to Shamil's side and bowed.

"The Infidel army has been sighted seven miles to the east. They will be here by dawn," he reported.

Before Shamil could reply, the muezzin's call to prayer floated from the minaret above them. The village paused in silence to listen.

Shamil nodded to himself, as if acknowledging some whispered message inaudible to mere mortal men. "It is the will of Allah," he said softly, and then cried out to his people, "We are prepared for battle! The outcome rests in the hands of Allah!"

"*La Allah illa Allahi!*" cried Hassan, and the prayer was taken up and echoed across the peaks. "Shamil Imam! There is none but Shamil!" called Hassan, and the village repeated the words fervently. Shamil then raised his hand and by that slight gesture brought a silence deeper than before. Then, taking Jemal-Edin by the hand, he led the men to the mosque for evening prayers.

IN THE HOUSES OF AKHULGO, AS IN ALL THE HOUSES
Jemal-Edin had ever seen, there was neither lamp nor
candle. Oil and tallow were far too precious to burn
merely for the luxury of seeing in the dark. When
night came, people went to bed; when daylight returned, they got up.

But on this dark night Jemal-Edin had a hard time
going to sleep. Beside him on the felt mats carpeting
the tiny room, Kazi Mohammed slept peacefully, un-
disturbed by the footsteps and clanking sabers in the
darkness outside the low window. Sometimes the
harsh whisper of men's voices could be heard. Dogs
barked. Once there was a great commotion of footsteps and women's wailing. He heard his mother slip
from the room to investigate.

"What is it?" he whispered anxiously to her.

"Sh-h-h. Do not wake your brother. I will return."
She spoke from the darkness above him. He waited

for what seemed a long, long time before she came back, her presence in the room visible only by a moving shadow darker than the night on the white walls.

"What was it?" he asked again as she lay down with a sigh and the rustle of the comforter she covered herself with.

"Refugees coming in from a village to the east."

"Many?"

"A long line of them—someone said more than nine hundred."

"Where will they sleep?"

"Shamil had them taken up to the old part of the town."

"Will Father come here to sleep tonight?" Suddenly the boy felt unsafe.

"No. He is busy with the Naibs and warriors."

"Oh."

"Go to sleep, my son. Morning will come all too soon."

"Mother?"

"Yes?"

"Are you afraid?"

"The Imam Shamil in his strength and wisdom will protect us. Have faith," was all she said. It was dogma, not an answer, and it gave no comfort.

"Yes, Mother," he said and squirmed stealthily under his blanket. Maybe if he could get the lumps out of his mat, he would feel better. But sleep eluded him. He kept thinking of all the things he had been shown and told that day, remembering the long dark corridors of stone which lay beneath the rock, beneath this very house; the supplies for a long siege; all the warriors—more men than he had ever seen in one place before—the prison pits with their cruelly spiked tops, empty now and waiting. Somewhere in the shadowed valleys below a huge army was crawling through the night, toward the village, toward them all. And although he believed his father was the greatest and most powerful man in the world, he felt uneasy. When he finally fell asleep, it was to dream bad dreams.

He was wakened in the dim light of morning by his mother's hand on his shoulder.

"Get dressed. Your father wants you with him."

As the boy rubbed the seeds of sleep from his eyes and looked at her, he was surprised to see she wore her finest clothing. She had on her long skirt and tight bodice of black velvet, her belt of heavy silver coins. Tucked into her belt was her best dagger with a hilt of jade and gold. The veil that exposed only her dark eyes, the ribbons that bound back her long black hair, all clinked with coins. Her eyes were outlined with kohl and above them her eyebrows met in an exaggerated pair of black swoops.

"One meets one's enemy with pride," she answered his unspoken question. "Hurry. Hassan waits for you."

Jemal-Edin pushed back the covers and shivered in the cold air even though he had slept in his pants and jacket. A second shiver shook his thin body and he scrambled to his feet and hurried over to urinate in the lavatory pit in the corner of the room. A brown spider, sluggish with cold but disturbed by the splashing, decided to move to a more sheltered corner. Spotting the hapless creature's movement, Jemal-Edin aimed at it and hosed it down the hole with a sense of satisfaction.

By the time he had put on his boots, goat hair cloak, and dagger belt, his mother had his morning meal ready; yogurt and bread with the crust soaked in sheep fat. He was too excited to eat, and in a few minutes he was out the door, almost running to keep up with the strides of Hassan who led the way up the hill.

There were still a few stars in the lightening sky. Clouds drifted over the mountains, obscuring the peaks around the village, moved overhead, and then were blown on by the sharp breeze. Jemal-Edin pulled his lambskin hat down over his ears.

From the distance came the sound of shots, sharp sporadic firings echoing and re-echoing off the cliffs. With each shot the boy's excitement heightened.

Shamil was with his officers in the gatehouse watchtower. Although he apparently had had no sleep, he looked both rested and immaculate, his henna-red beard carefully trimmed, his Imam's turban with its fresh red ribbons gleaming above the black hat. He was scanning the defiles below with a telescope when Jemal-Edin entered. Minutes passed while he continued his observations and gave no acknowledgment of his son's presence. Then he abruptly handed the instrument to the boy without looking at him.

"They are attempting to take the path," he said.

It took Jemal-Edin a moment for his sight to focus

through the telescope. Then he could see them. Men in gray-green uniforms were marching in a long line —like an endless centipede winding its way up the mountain. Little white puffs of smoke spouted here and there along the line marking those who stopped to fire. Now and then one would fall and another would kneel quickly beside the fallen man, victim of Shamil's snipers hidden on surrounding cliffs. As Jemal-Edin watched, the advance column reached the first rock barricade across the path. The soldiers piled forward in an attempt to scale it. From the trenches below came a quick volley of shots. The Russian soldiers fell almost to a man.

Shamil grabbed back the telescope to see how his men were doing. Jemal-Edin found he could see the fight clearly without any aid. Time and time again the Russian column tried to move forward, now over the mounting bodies of their own wounded that blocked the path. With no shelter along the rock wall above the river, they were nearly helpless against the guns of Shamil.

"It is like shooting targets," Hassan remarked.

"Allah is kind to us by making the Russian general stupid," said another, and Jemal-Edin smiled with appreciation.

"But not so kind, perhaps, to the men who must obey those officers," commented Shamil and he did not smile.

By the time the sun came up the bodies of Russian dead could be seen scattered for half a mile along the cliffs. A trumpet sounded. Men began sliding down to the river on ropes, dropping off, and starting to swim across. The current took them sideways and downstream, but most made it to the other side and disappeared under the peak on which the village stood.

"They are going to try to scale the cliffs," Shamil announced almost sadly. "Alert the women." A Naib hurried off, his saber slapping against his boots.

"While the warriors harass the soldiers on the opposite cliff, our women will drop stones and roll burning logs down on those attempting to climb up from below," Shamil explained to his son. "Not only does this spare our men, but it lets the Infidel know that even the weakest of our women can defeat them. Come. We shall watch."

Disdainful of the chance that a Russian sniper might pick him off, and secure with both his faith and his bodyguards surrounding him, Shamil led the way through the village. The people, joyous now that the waiting was over and they could fight again, felt sure of winning. They greeted his presence with glad shouts that drowned out the screams of the Russian soldiers being knocked off the cliffs they were attempting to scale.

All day long Jemal-Edin walked the fortress with his father, highly visible in his white clothes, not only to his father's people, but to the soldiers of the Infidel. The boy watched the women as they lugged stones from the huge piles by the trenches that rimmed the outer bastions and rolled the rocks down the sides of the hill. The lines of Russian troops moving up from the ravines below grew greater and greater until they seemed to be everywhere. But they were below, in the open, exposed, and shooting upward with inadequate guns against well-armed enemies hidden behind stone walls.

When the fighting stopped at nightfall, a Naib came to report to Shamil that more than three hundred and fifty Russian soldiers were counted dead, more than two thousand wounded. Akhulgo's only casualty was a woman who had tripped on her hem and fallen over the edge of the cliff to her death.

When Jemal-Edin woke the next morning, it was to the usual village sounds—crowing roosters and his mother moving about in the outer room preparing the morning meal. There were no slaves at Akhulgo; Shamil wanted no extra mouths to feed, no person he could not trust.

The quiet lasted almost a week. The Russians had pulled back their men, away from the ferocious defense of the fortress, out of range from both gunfire and falling debris. Instead they were now engaged in building three heavy bridges across the river. To protect their engineers and workmen from Murid sharpshooters, they stationed deep lines of infantrymen up and down both sides of the stream.

Although Shamil's guerrillas harassed them constantly, the bridges were nearly completed. Then a band of Murids, their faces blackened with soot, their black clothing blending into the night, crept down from the cliffs and into the river to float downstream beneath the bridges. They towed with them hides filled with naphtha. The whole village turned out to stand on the rooftops and cheer the flames from the burning Infidel bridges.

Still Akhulgo remained quiet. There was occasional firing from the army now encamped below, but it was half-hearted. The Murid night-fighters went down the cliff each night and returned at dawn, their numbers undiminished but notches in their daggers marked the number of throats they had slit in the darkness.

Jemal-Edin spent the days with his father, listening to strategy, hearing the reports of messengers who came and left the village encampment almost ignored by the enemy. The grim and ascetic Murids at first ignored the boy, then were bemused by his constant presence, and finally came to cheer at his appearance beside Shamil.

"Why do they do that?" Jemal-Edin once, in flattered confusion, asked his father.

"They regard you as a good omen," said Shamil, "as I intended them to do. So long as you are with me, they believe we are all safe."

There were times in the midst of long sessions when Jemal-Edin listened wistfully to the shouts of boys his age as they played. Although the boys of this village were strangers to him, still he longed for their company. But he never complained. His duty now was to be with his father. Duty came first for a man.

Long days passed in waiting until the people began to question why they waited. Why didn't Shamil strike now?

There came a night in early July when several hundred Murids, men Jemal-Edin had not seen before, suddenly appeared over the edge of the cliffside and made their way to Shamil's quarters next door to the mosque. They had been unable to cut off the Russian army, their Naib officers reported to Shamil. Many villages had deserted, frightened of Russian vengeance. The rest had been razed by Cossacks, all the inhabitants killed. Infidel troops filled the uplands around Akhulgo, commanded all approaches to the fortress. Still more troops were arriving in countless numbers in the valley. They were bringing with them long lines of supply wagons and many cannon. Akhulgo was surrounded. The Russians meant to win, to end this war.

WITH THE FIRST LIGHT OF MORNING A CANNON BALL
sheered off the top of the minaret. It crashed, killing
the muezzin, a dog, and two chickens. The old muezzin's scream as he fell was the first death cry of Akhulgo.

Shamil himself came to the house to see that both
his wives and Kazi Mohammed went immediately to
the rock shelters. Once sure that his family was safe,
he took Jemal-Edin with him to the command blockhouse. From this vantage point the boy could see
across to the bluffs above them.

During the night, and obviously for many nights
before, the Russians had been busily dragging heavy
cannon up the cliffs with men used as dray animals.
Horses and mules could not be forced up such terrify-
ingly steep inclines. One big gun was already in position, aimed down at Akhulgo. Four more were being
readied for firing. Hundreds of Russian soldiers

swarmed over the peaks, pulling with great effort the immense iron-wheeled cannon mounts, and tugging fat mortars up the rock faces.

Shamil's spies reported that the Murid forces were now outnumbered one hundred to one by the army of the Great White Sultan. But snug in his fortress, these reports did not dismay Shamil. He knew the czar's love of tradition was the Murid's best ally.

The czar armed his men with old-fashioned flint-lock muskets. Designed for fusillades against massed infantry at close range, these guns were smoothbore weapons loaded at the muzzle with gunpowder, and then with a single large ball which had to be pushed down the barrel by a ramrod. Pulling the trigger caused a flint to strike against steel and the resulting spark ignited the powder, causing an explosion which sent the steel ball flying perhaps one hundred yards. Regardless of the fact that a well-trained infantryman could load and fire his musket four times a minute, his weapon put the individual Russian soldier at a severe disadvantage against the better-armed Murid war-riors.

Shamil, being desperate, couldn't afford the luxury of tradition. From modern English rifles captured in Turkish raids, he had the Daghestani armorers pain-stakingly tool handmade copies. These were true rifles, guns with spiral grooves rifled into the barrel to im-part a spin to the ball, giving it much greater speed, accuracy, and twice the range of a musket against game the size of a man. These guns were .45 caliber cartridge breech-loading sharpshooters and the Murids could fire as fast as they could load. As the warriors fired, the empty cartridge cases were picked up by the children who raced them back to the women to be reloaded and returned to the ammunition supply points.

Hidden behind their stone battlements, the Murids shot mark, picking off the victim of their choice, taking time to aim carefully so that no shot was wasted. But for each Russian they killed, ten more appeared to take his place. Against the Murids' punishing gunfire the mounting of the cannon continued, even though more Russians were soon engaged in carrying away the wounded and dying than in returning fire.

It was imperative that the Russians stay out of rifle range. Yet still they were ordered to mount the cannon. To refuse such an order would have resulted in death by the guns of their own officers and so they obeyed. Some of them walked cliffs so high and so sheer that the men were made dizzy by the altitude and fear. Some slipped and fell to their deaths without being shot while their companions clung to the rock face and watched in horror. But in the face of such fear, the army persisted in mounting more cannon until the fortress of Akhulgo below them was encircled.

When the cannon began to fire in unison, their great roars of explosion reverberated through the ravines. The outer walls of the fortress fell against the blast. The rubble crushed several hundred warriors in the trenches beneath the walls.

In the underground stables Jemal-Edin could hear the few remaining horses screaming and stamping in terror. From somewhere to the south came the screams of women and frightened babies. Commanding his son to stay in the blockhouse, Shamil left with his officers, hurrying to rally his men.

Encouraged by the toppled walls, the Russians once again tried to storm their way up to the fortress. They met with furious firing and had to fall back. Akhulgo, buried in her rock, was still very much alive.

For the next week the bombardment from the surrounding peaks continued nonstop. Death rained down on the village day and night. But while the surface buildings were leveled to rubble, in the tunnels below, the people continued to live and fight back.

Under cover of darkness Shamil had the wounded evacuated down the cliff and taken to other villages by trails still unknown to the enemy. Fresh troops and supplies came into Akhulgo the same way, under the noses of Russian sentries. But time and effort could not be spared for the dead.

The dead were many and lay in open trenches. There was no place to bury them in the rock. Religion forbade throwing them over the cliff edge. With the sun the dead became Akhulgo's most terrible enemy. The wells and cistern were slowly buried under rubble and contaminated. Typhoid began to take its toll, then cholera. In the hot July afternoons ravens and vultures began their remorseless circling above the peak, sometimes swooping to land on a body only to be driven off by a screaming woman taking this final care of her dead warrior or child.

Jemal-Edin moved through this nightmare with Shamil. All excitement was gone from the boy now

and had been since the day he saw Faizil crushed by
a cannon ball meant for the Imam—and saw his father walk on as if nothing had happened. From then
on he walked dazed through the rubble and stench.
Shamil was taking desperate chances, still appearing
openly with his son, both now dressed in white,
which made them excellent targets for the sniper fire
which somehow never hit them. He was trying every
way he knew to encourage and inspire his army. But
Shamil was losing and Jemal-Edin knew it. And so did
the Murid warriors.

The Russian general, thinking his enemy was at last
defeated when two days finally passed with no response from the fortress, sent a column of six hundred
troops up the cliffside. They were armed with muskets and carried scaling ladders and ropes. From what
they thought to be a blank cliff face came a barrage of
gunfire, riddling them, trapping them there exposed
and unable to retreat or continue upward. They had
found the blockhouse Jemal-Edin had spied that day
when Shamil had shown him the defenses.

Another column coming up the other side ran into a
legion of women and children, maddened with grief
and fury, who trapped them on a ledge and bombarded them with boulders and burning brands, then
finished off the wounded with their daggers. The children, being shorter, rushed forward toward the line
and slashed upward beneath the fixed bayonets of the
Russian soldiers, who could not believe little children
were dangerous. When the children were killed, the
mothers used the bodies as weapons by throwing

them at the soldiers, forcing them to fall backwards over the cliff edge—the mothers falling with the children in death.

Furious cannon fire followed. The blockhouse at the gate, having been located by the deaths of the six hundred, was blasted to bits. The living quarters, spotted by the exodus of women attacking the other line, were also bombarded. And then the shelling stopped and silence returned to the mountains. Days passed, each one sunnier and hotter than the last, until the stench of the dying village almost overwhelmed the army camped below it.

Once the shelling stopped, Shamil spent all his time in the ruined mosque. Of the original complement of Naibs who had been his personal escort, only Hassan remained alive. Most of the men of Akhulgo over the age of twelve were dead. Those remaining were suffering from dehydration and starvation, wounds and extreme fatigue.

In the quiet, women and children emerged from the darkness of the underground hiding places. Among them were Kazi Mohammed and his mother, Fatimat. It was she who first laid aside her dagger and began silently to build an oven from the rubble of the ruined houses. Somewhere she found flour and a goat to milk and made bread. Other women joined to help her, or sat in the sun to mend what clothing they had left, or sharpen their daggers. The children, reassured by these signs of a return to normalcy, began to play behind the barricades or explore this strangeness that had once been their home.

Jemal-Edin, as always, was with his father. Whether

on the ramparts or in the ruined blockhouses or at prayer in the mosque, he was where duty and his father's command ordered, one pace behind Shamil. Not a warrior but only a white shadow.

In the still heat of the afternoon a small band of warriors from a distant village rode under a white banner through the Russian lines up the narrow defile to Akhulgo. They signaled their wish to parley and were permitted to advance on foot to the fortress. They were met by Hassan who spoke with them for some time.

"The Starshina of Tchirkei is acting as an intermediary for the Infidel, General Grabbé," Hassan reported to Shamil, who waited in the mosque.

"Tchirkei is a village of traitors and their chieftain is the greatest among them!" snapped Shamil, his face gaunt and pale, his eyes shining with exhaustion and anger. "If they had not surrendered, the others might not have and we would not be trapped here. You have my permission to cleave him to the waist with your saber."

"Yes, Most Honored Imam," Hassan acknowledged the permission with a bow, "but first perhaps you should hear what terms they offer?"

Shamil waited in haughty silence for the man to continue.

"I repeat only what the Starshina said to me," Hassan said, carefully prefacing his remarks to avoid Shamil's wrath. "The White Sultan's general demands your complete surrender to his government, along with all arms and warriors. And as a mark of your good intentions, demands in addition, that you send to his camp your first-born son, Jemal-Edin, who is to remain with the enemy until final negotiations are complete."

Shamil now fixed his terrible gaze upon his officer, and stepped toward him. His hand reached automatically for his dagger, but then stayed itself, as he remembered that it was not his loyal Hassan who made this request, but his enemies. He stalked away, back to the interior of the ruined mosque where one shining brass lamp still hung askew from a charred rafter, then back to where Hassan waited for his reply.

For the first time in his life Jemal-Edin was aware of being afraid of his father. All through the siege fear had clutched his insides, a fear he could never admit because an Avar was never afraid. Shamil had told him so. The shots, the mortars, the cannon balls, the noise, the stench, and death—the fear of all that seemed inconsequential to the fear he felt now. What if Shamil sent him to the hated enemy?

"You tell the traitor there is only one reason Allah lets him leave here with his life," Shamil's voice was thick with bitterness and hatred. "So that he may take my message back to the White Sultan's general. I will not surrender! I will never surrender so long as I have breath to fight! And tell the traitor the day will come when he and I meet. On that day he will die and his corpse will feed the vultures!"

The emissaries left the fortress soon after. Jemal-Edin watched in relief as they went. He thought the shelling would recommence when the Russians received his father's reply. But it did not. There was occasional sniper fire from the peaks above and the shots were returned by Shamil's men, but most days were passed in silent waiting.

After another week the last of the food was gone. The Russians had succeeded in cutting off any passage into or out of the fortress. The ammunition was almost gone. The dead were still with them. Now the remaining warriors prayed openly for death. Shamil could no longer inspire them. There was no way left for them to fight, and they prayed that the enemy would attack so they could die honorably, in battle, with a saber in their hands. The starving women and children kept up a ceaseless wail. In the mosque Jemal-Edin prayed with his father for the mercy of Allah.

ON AUGUST 18, 1839, SHAMIL HIMSELF RAISED A WHITE flag on the remains of the shattered minaret. The siege of Àkhulgo was ended.

An hour later a small complement of Russian officers rode into the village. Before they could dismount two men slipped from their horses in a faint, overcome by the stench of the place. After watching Hassan greet the men, Shamil sent Jemal-Edin from the mosque.

"Go to your mother," he said. "I will send for you."

Jemal-Edin had not seen his mother for many days. Her fine clothing was torn and dirty almost beyond recognition, her eyes very large in her thin face and bright, as if she had been weeping. When he came into the underground room where she and Kazi were staying with Javaret and the baby, she greeted him quietly and told him to remove his clothing.

"You must bathe," she said, "and put on your best.

The son of Shamil will greet the officers of the White Sultan looking like the noble he is."

From somewhere a small jar of water was produced and the boy, feeling very guilty to waste something so precious for the mere reason of getting clean, washed himself with her help. When he was finished, she dressed him as she had done when he was small. Somehow in the midst of the destruction and desolation, she had managed to keep for him his finest suit of clothes. The white woolen pants and the jacket with its cartridge cases over the chest, the long coat of finest wool and the high white lambskin hat—all were immaculate. There were even new boots of cream-colored kid.

Shamil himself came into the cavelike room as Jemal-Edin was fastening on his belt and dagger. The Imam stood darkening the doorway, looking down at his son. The boy saw that his father's normally unexpressive face was twisted with grief and bitterness.

"What is it?" he asked before thinking. "What is wrong?"

Shamil waved back the warriors and Hassan who would have followed him into the tiny room. The Imam knelt on one knee before his son.

"So that Akhulgo may live, you must be brave," he said heavily. "You are the son of Shamil. You must be proud and above reproach. The Infidels demand that I give you up as hostage while the negotiations are made. If I do not, they will kill everyone here. Our people have suffered enough. They must not all die but must live so that they may regain their strength and fight again—so that Daghestan may live! Only you can give them the chance to do that now, my son."

It took Jemal-Edin a moment to understand what his father was saying, so alarmed was he to see the great man kneeling before him, openly defeated and grieving.

"I am to go to the Infidels?" he asked, not quite believing it, and yet knowing with sickening certainty it was true.

"If you wish to save our lives, yes," nodded Shamil.

"It is my duty to do this?" His hands and feet went cold.

"It is my wish and Allah's will if we are to survive."

From behind him he heard his mother choke back a sob and felt his own throat tighten. Kazi rushed forward and threw his arms around his brother and began to cry. "Don't go, Jemal-Edin! Don't go!"

"Your brother is a man," Shamil said gently, pulling the little boy away and holding him with one long arm. "You must leave him free to make his own decision." And then to his first son, he said, "When you are with the Infidels, you must behave with honor. You must not weep. Not now or later! You must act with patience as well as courage. You must not use your dagger on them, but endure the insult of their unclean touch. It will not be for long. They have promised me you will be kept at Tchirkei." And seeing the boy still hesitate, he added, "Only in this manner can you save my life so that I may go on leading our people to freedom."

Jemal-Edin looked into his father's eyes and saw tears there. It was the tears more than anything else that made him nod his head. "I will go," he said sadly. "But I do not think they will let me come back," and his voice nearly broke.

"It will not be for long," Shamil assured him, his manner easier now. "The time will come soon again when you will be beside me, riding through our mountains, on your own stallion instead of a small horse, and I shall give you the saber of a man. Together we will fight the Infidels again, and together we shall defeat them!"

Jemal-Edin nodded dumbly. Somehow all that did not seem important anymore. He turned to his mother.

"You will say your farewells in here," Shamil ordered quickly. "Pride is all I have left to me. I will not have the nobles or the village see my family weep."

Fatimat knelt quickly and Jemal-Edin silently hugged her for the last time. Her body felt tight and trembling. Then Kazi Mohammed, who did not want to let go of him. Jemal-Edin's eyes burned, and he was blinking back tears. An Avar does not cry, he kept repeating to himself. Then he turned to embrace his father who lifted him up and hugged him fiercely, kissing him on both cheeks.

Out in the sunlight the elite of Shamil's surviving nobles, led by Hassan, waited to escort him from Akhulgo. The Russian officers had left the fortress before, as a matter of honor, waiting to see if Shamil would keep his word.

Under the black Murid banners carried by the men, the boy walked alone, erect and proud as his father would wish. Out of the ruined gate, down the rubble-strewn path toward the hated Russians. At the remains of the last barricade the Naib escort stopped. Jemal-Edin walked on by himself, a small white figure against the background of bloodstained cliffs.

Looking up to the shattered ramparts of the fortress, he could see the survivors of the village gathering to watch him leave. As word spread of his going, a wailing prayer to Allah rose on the breathless August air, begging for his protection and return. His mother stood apart from the other women, her veiled face buried in her hands. He saw Kazi Mohammed running along the cliff, crying desperately and calling "Come back, Jemal-Edin! Come back! Oh please, come back!" And in the background, like a recitative, he could hear his father intoning a prayer of vengeance for this insult to the Imam's dignity and honor.

At the arranged meeting point, two Russian staff officers waited for him. They came forward, smiling, holding out their pale hands in greeting. But the boy turned away. Not in sullenness, but so that they could not see the silent tears running down his face. An Avar does not cry, he kept repeating to himself, feeling their big hands grasp his shoulders and lead him along.

Behind him on the path the black Murid banners fluttered and dipped in a final farewell salute. And now, at last, Shamil appeared on the roof of the mosque. But Jemal-Edin, his head down to hide the shame of the tears, did not look back again.

SEVERAL HUNDRED YARDS AHEAD, BEYOND THE RANGE OF possible Murid sniper fire, the trio was met by a formal military escort who conducted the young hostage down the long path into the canyon encampment and up to the command tent of General Grabbé.

Although he could not understand the Infidel's language, Jemal-Edin knew from the deference shown this scowling fat man in the medal-encrusted uniform that he was a great chieftain. The general was sitting behind a heavy wooden table strewn with maps and papers. He did not bother to rise as Jemal-Edin was shown in.

"Most High Excellency, General Grabbé, may I present your hostage, Jemal-Edin, first son of Shamil the Avar, Imam of Daghestan . . ."

"I know who the brat is," growled the general impatiently. "So far as I'm concerned he's an offspring of the devil." He condescended to glance at the boy who was watching him with hatred. "I see he is as arrogant as the fanatic who sired him."

"He is reportedly of noble blood, Most High Excellency," remarked an officer standing behind the general.

The general spat on the rich rug of the tent floor. Jemal-Edin could not understand the words, but the insult was very clear. The boy clenched his hands tightly against his sides, his palms itching to pull his dagger and remove the sneer from the face of this fat Infidel. Only his father's remembered command not to use the knife restrained him.

"They all claim to be noble, these Tartar peasants, the sons of great khans. They live in stone hovels, pray on their bellies. All they have to their misbegotten names are their stallions, their sabers, and their damnable arrogance. For thirty years we have wasted our time trying to pacify them, to build roads, to bring them the benefits of civilization. For thirty years they have defied us! I intend to end it!" The general struck the table with his fist. "Now! Once and for all time! Look at him . . ." he gestured toward the boy, "the insufferable arrogance of them all! We reduce his fortress to rubble, and Shamil still thinks he can dictate terms to me! I'll see him in chains on his way to the mines!"

As though suddenly aware he was shouting, General Grabbé stopped and took a deep breath, then resumed speaking with greater calm. "It must be clear to you, gentlemen, that I have no intention of honoring any terms made with the brigand Shamil. I will accept nothing but total subjugation. The hostage is to be taken to the commander in chief. From there he will be sent to St. Petersburg. Your orders are prepared. A carriage is waiting. You are dismissed."

A few minutes later, Jemal-Edin found himself wedged on the warm leather carriage seat between the stocky forms of Captains Vlastov and Von Cernea. They were the same two officers who had come to meet him on the path from Akhulgo. The driver slapped the reins over the backs of the team and they lurched off along the river through the huge field camp.

It was early evening. The soldiers were relaxing for the first time in more than a month, rejoicing in the cease-fire, celebrating around the campfires in front of their tents. As the carriage passed among them, Jemal-Edin could hear snatches of music from strange instruments and the deep voices of Cosssacks singing. The air smelled of woodsmoke and roasting meat, crushed earth, and grass. Very different smells from the stench of Akhulgo.

He felt lightheaded from nerve strain and lack of food. He had never ridden in a carriage before. The motion was unfamiliar and upsetting to him. For a time he watched the broad back of the driver on the seat ahead, the bob and pitch of the horses' heads as they trotted along. The iron-rimmed wheels of the carriage jarred up and down over the rocks, the seat box swayed on tortured springs. Ahead and behind the carriage rode guard details, and he envied them the familiar comfort of their saddles.

The officers spoke Russian, French, and German, but no Arabic. They could not communicate with the boy. But tense as he was, Jemal-Edin realized they were trying to be kind. They offered him strange fruit and sweets, bread and cheese. He shook his head in refusal. Not only was the food defiled by the touch of Infidel hands, but he knew if he ate anything, he would throw up, and he could not endure the thought of such humiliation in front of his enemies.

After repeated tries to get him to eat, the men gave up, ate most of the food themselves, and settled back, arms folded, to enjoy as best they could the long ride through the mountains.

By nightfall the carriage had reached the timber line and the first of the wind-stunted pines appeared alongside the military road. As they descended, the clear air became sweet with the scent of fir needles crushed beneath the wheels. With night and the trees, the temperature dropped. For the first time Jemal-Edin felt free from sweat inside his woolen clothing. He unconsciously sighed with relief and settled back more comfortably between his two affable guards. He saw the men exchange a look and smile as he did this, but he ignored them. He was too tired to care what anyone did anymore.

"The boy seems to be quieting down a little," said Captain Vlastov who sat on Jemal-Edin's right, regarding him as he would an attractive, but dangerous, wild animal.

"I am relieved to see it. He was wound tight in Grabbé's tent. I kept wondering if we should take that knife from him. I had the uncomfortable impression he was going to use it when the general spat."

"Do you think he understood what was said?"

"If nothing else, he understood the name of his father."

Captain Vlastov nodded, and then after some thought asked, "Did you ever see his father?"

"No. Never. But then has anyone? Any Russian? There are times when I think the man just another mountain myth, like the djinns and fire monsters."

"I saw him once," said Vlastov rather proudly.

"No! Where?"

"Some years ago—at the battle of Gimri. Of course I did not know it was he until after it was all over."

At the mention of his birthplace, Jemal-Edin looked up at Captain Vlastov. The man smiled down at him and patted him warily on the top of his furry white hat. "You go to sleep, boy," he suggested uselessly and went on telling his story to the other man. But though he tried to listen, Jemal-Edin heard no words he understood other than the repeated name of Gimri.

"Gimri is like all their village fortresses, stone buildings on top of a mountain. The trail to it runs for more than twenty miles around the peak. Until Akhulgo, I had never seen or imagined a place of human habitation so desolate. Nothing green grows up there. No trees. No grass. Not even moss." Vlastov shook his head in wonder thinking of it. "I have never understood how they live."

"Very poorly, from what I have seen," commented Von Cernea, "but do go on with your story."

"The trail up is so narrow and the drop so sheer we had to blindfold our horses to make them move. It was almost as bad with the men on foot. They were terrified, and I can't say I blamed them. Twenty miles of that! We had hundreds of contusion casualties, men who were made dizzy by fear of the height and simply fell.

"It was the first time we used cannon on a high fortress and the Murids weren't prepared for it. Once we had the guns mounted on the cliffs above, the battle lasted only a day more." He grunted to himself with satisfaction as he recalled, "By then, reinforcements had joined us. It was ten thousand of us to five hundred of them. They knew they were doomed, but they would not surrender. We had to go in for hand-to-hand fighting. The Murids lashed themselves together in human chains so if one fell, the next could hold him up. Then they started coming out under white flags, pretending to surrender. But when they were close to our infantry, old men, women, even children would draw their daggers and slash out."

Vlastov fell silent, thinking of that night and its terrible toll in human life.

"When one recalls that Medea was born in the Caucasus, it becomes easier to understand both her character and theirs," Von Cernea observed. "But to get back to the boy's father—you said he was there?"

"He was the only man who escaped. We knew his name then, but no one knew much about him other than that he was the second in command to Imam Kazi Mohammed, and had a reputation as a holy man.

"When we had taken all the fortress except for two stone blockhouses, the order came to retreat and shelling recommenced. By the time it stopped it was nearly midnight. We advanced again in complete silence. There was no more sniper fire from the blockhouses. We thought everybody inside was dead. Then, without any warning, a very tall man all dressed in black appeared in the doorframe of what had been the biggest blockhouse. His face was dead white in the light of the flames, and the look in his eyes..."

The listening driver had slowed the team in order to hear better over the rumble of the wheels, and now, as Vlastov stopped speaking for a moment, the cry of a night bird curled up from somewhere in the darkness of the forest.

"For a moment he simply stood there, as if daring us to shoot. Four of my men were near him. They stared up at him as if they had lost their wits. By the time they remembered to aim, he moved—in one tremendous leap over their heads, he landed, whirled about and killed three of them with one slash of his saber! The fourth man managed to bayonet him. They stood for an instant face to face until Shamil backed off from the blade. I could see he was bleeding badly, but he wrenched the bayonet away from my poor devil, killed him with it and two more men who rushed up. Then he took a running leap, cleared a seven-foot wall and disappeared into the night."

"Incredible!" Von Cernea said with a low whistle of disbelief.

"But, as God is my witness, it is all true!"

"And your men failed to track down someone so badly wounded?"

"Oh, we tried, but to be quite honest, I doubt if any man there, officer or otherwise, truly wanted to find him in the dark." Vlastov grunted a half-apologetic laugh. "In my lifetime I have met only two men whose very presence frightened me—Czar Nicholas and Shamil! I will never forget the look on his face!"

Von Cernea laughed rather uneasily. "My dear Vlastov, you were probably exhausted, suffering from a case of nerves . . . and now that you have heard some of the myths circulating about the man, you may tend to forget what really happened that night."

"No. I don't think so," Vlastov said. "There are some people who believe so strongly in their destiny that they make others believe it. And sometimes it is difficult to doubt. Why, for example, of all who died at Gimri, was he the only man to escape? And by doing so, live on to become their Imam?"

"He was obviously the better soldier," said Von Cernea. "From what you said, he was stronger, quicker, smarter, more disciplined. And perhaps—just plain lucky."

"Perhaps . . . or was it his destiny?"

"We make our own destiny," said Von Cernea. "And I suspect you have been on this campaign too long. A few more years out here in this beautiful, Godforsaken mountain country and you will become as superstitious as the natives."

"Perhaps." The other man shrugged and his voice lightened. "Shall we change the topic of conversation? Since we must stay awake to guard our passenger here, we might as well enjoy it. Bring out that bottle of wine there under the opposite seat. We will drink to the full moon and discuss more pleasant things."

"Like Count Nirod's five beautiful Persian mistresses?"

"Exactly! Did you say 'five'? There is a man who obviously has a destiny one could envy!"

Jemal-Edin, who was falling asleep, was momentarily wakened by the guffaws of ribald laughter. He wondered what his father would say if he could see him now, being driven through the night, flanked by Infidels who were smoking the abhorred tobacco and drinking the abhorred wine. And not only that, but pouring a glassful of the wine and giving it to the slave who drove them! They were strange men, these enemies. They seemed friendly, they laughed, they had not once hit him, they indulged in all the forbidden weaknesses, yet they appeared strong. Perhaps this was their evil way of putting him off his guard, so that he would suffer more when they put him into their prison pits.

As he slipped back into sleep the boy slumped to the left and the Russian officer obligingly turned sideways to provide a more comfortable pillow of his thigh. The other man reached behind the seat and fished around in the darkness to come up with a robe which he draped over Jemal-Edin.

11

AFTER A GOOD NIGHT'S SLEEP DESPITE THE BUMPY RIDE, Jemal-Edin was feeling far stronger when the carriage pulled up in front of the commander in chief's head-quarters at the valley garrison town of Temir-Khan-Shura. They had no more than stopped when they were surrounded by Russian and Cossack soldiers—men curious to see the son of Shamil, men who crowded around, laughing, pointing, talking in their strange tongues.

Jemal-Edin felt like a dwarf slave he had once seen at Dargo, a thing to be made sport of. He was the son of Shamil! How dare they treat him this way!

The officers stepped down from the carriage, grate-ful the long ride was over. Von Cernea reached in to assist Jemal-Edin to the ground. Jemal-Edin drew back his hands, folded them tightly over his chest and sat, face taut and white with fury. He was not going to move!

Von Cernea shrugged, stepped up again into the carriage and picked him up bodily, only to find he had picked up a bundle of rage. Jemal-Edin squirmed out of the man's surprised grasp and leaped over the side of the carriage, drawing his dagger as he jumped. As the wicked-looking long knife flashed in the sun, there was suddenly a wide circle around him as men tripped backwards to get away from this wild little warrior.

He danced in an ever-widening circle, knife slashing the air. As soon as he saw a break in the ranks of the startled but laughing men, he burst through it and ran down the street. There were trees on the hills. If he could reach them . . . But he was too weak to run far. A tall blond-haired guard in red caught up with him and roughly grabbed his arm, breaking his grip on the dagger. As it fell, the giant scooped him up and carried him, kicking and screaming Avar insults, back to the two captains. They hustled him off, one firm hand under each of his arms, up onto the porch and inside the building. The laughter of his enemies followed him all the way. He wanted to die from the shame of it.

The room was large, like the exterior, its walls were painted the muted red that designated all military property of the czar. A map covered one wall. Clustered around the map stood a great number of staff officers of various rank. Mixed among them were native interpreters and chieftains of clans who had gone over to the Russian side.

Jemal-Edin stared in wonder at all the bright uniforms, the medals and gold braid the men wore. He forgot some of his rage. A tall, very handsome man with a magnificent mustache separated himself from the group at the map and came over to the boy. He wore a green Russian uniform with many medals and a spotless white turban decorated with a very large emerald. This gem more than anything else told the boy the man was a very powerful sultan.

"I see you frightened our brave soldiers," he said in the Avar tongue. His lips curled in a sardonic smile.

They were the first words Jemal-Edin had understood since he left Akhulgo. He looked at the man with surprise, but no less hatred. If the man spoke his language, then he was a Daghestani and a traitor . . . or he would not be in this accursed place.

"There is no need of more violence, boy. We are not going to hurt you. Do you understand that?" When he received no reply, he went on, his tone sympathetic. "You are, of course, a hostage. But believe me, you will be well cared for. I know things look very bad for you right now. But they are not as bad as they seem. Once you can accept the idea, you will feel better. Please try to understand. The worst is over. I regret that General Grabbé felt it necessary to remove you from your family. But it is done. That cannot be changed. To make up for that loss, we have great plans for you. Do you want to hear them?"

Jemal-Edin showed him what he hoped was the same disdain he had seen his father express. The son of Shamil was not interested in the words of a traitor. Let them treat him as they willed, he would show the bravery of a warrior. Out of the corner of his eye he saw a guard walk over to the central desk and lay something on it. It was his dagger! He wished he had it back; he would give this fancy sultan something to talk about!

"Well, if you like it or not," the turbaned man continued, "you are to be sent north, to the great czar."

"But I am to go to the Tchirkei chieftain—to be kept there—my father said this!"

Jemal-Edin felt as if the ground had just shifted under his feet. The thought of being held captive in a neighboring village was bad enough. He could at least imagine what that would be like. He knew how his father treated captives. But the idea of being taken someplace completely strange, perhaps even stranger than this place he was in now . . .

"No. Your father is . . . mistaken. You will go where General Grabbé wishes," the sultan said firmly. "But do not be afraid. You will find it is not so bad at all. You will see wonderful things—have advantages you would not have here. On your journey north you will see much of Russia, visit her greatest cities—even live in one of them! And you will meet the Czar of All the Russias! Now don't you think you might like that?"

"No!" said Jemal-Edin.

The sultan shrugged. "As you wish," he said. "But I would advise you, if you do not wish to travel with your hands and feet bound, that you start acting like the gentleman your father would wish you to be."

For the first time something the sultan said got through to the boy. The man was right, Jemal-Edin thought, Shamil would not approve of the way he was behaving. It was not very dignified.

"They laughed at me," he said in his own defense. "They had no right to point and laugh. I am . . ."

"They are fools," said the tall man. "You should pay

them no attention. So long as a man knows his own worth, the opinion of others does not matter. I am sure your father has told you that?"

"My mother has."

"Good." The man started to turn away. "Remember what I told you," he repeated. "You have nothing to fear. It will be a little strange to you. But no one will harm you in any way—as long as you behave. And even if you do not believe me now—you will learn to. And you shall like what you see. I did."

"That is because they paid you well to betray your people," thought Jemal-Edin as he watched the tall sultan disappear into the same room the two captains had entered. But it was hard to remain angry and indignant when nobody paid any attention to him. He was left standing there in the corner of the big room, a rather disheveled little island in a sea of floor. Across the room the enemy officers talked and laughed and argued with each other. They had forgotten all about him. He might consider himself an important hostage, but these men were making it all too clear that they considered him, if at all, as nothing more than another barbarian child.

Some of his anger and fear ebbed away, and with it, his energy. He was tired and bewildered and, most of all, hungry. "What would they do if I just walked out?" he thought. He glanced quickly around the room to see if anyone were watching. Someone was.

Across the room a young lieutenant in a gray uniform met his glance and smiled. Jemal-Edin did not return the smile and pretended to be very interested in the view from the nearest window. Still he could see the young officer get up from his desk and go over to the central desk and pick up the dagger. He looked at it closely with obvious admiration, then slapped its hilt thoughtfully against his open palm. After a bit, he turned and crossed over to Jemal-Edin. He stopped directly in front of him, brought his heels together with a smart click, bowed and presented the knife to its owner.

No other gesture could have so effectively captured the boy's imagination. He was the child of warriors, raised by their code. For what the gesture said was: "You may be a captive, but you are a man whom we greatly respect. We know that when we return your weapon, you will have the honor not to betray our trust by using that weapon."

Jemal-Edin accepted the weapon gravely, then on impulse, attempted to click his heels and bow as the lieutenant had done. He succeeded only in kicking himself painfully in the left ankle and his face turned red with embarrassment. But the lieutenant did not smile. Jemal-Edin attempted the deep bow again. This time he did it right. As he sheathed the long knife, he thought how silly he must have looked when he kicked himself and a smile creased his face. The lieutenant smiled back at him. It was the first time Jemal-Edin had smiled in more than a month.

The young man called across to one of the senior officers and acknowledged the reply to his question with a jaunty salute. Then he turned to Jemal-Edin and held out his hand. After hesitating, the boy took it. The hand of this Infidel felt cool and dry and smelled of nothing worse than tobacco smoke. And contrary to what Jemal-Edin had always been taught, it was cleaner than most Murid hands. Even as he noted these things he felt more confused.

He was led from the room, along a dark corridor and into another room where rows of tables stood flanked by benches. On the tables were small samovars and glass vases with flowers and pine boughs. A soldier approached and the man spoke to him. The soldier left and then reappeared a moment later with a large tray that held cups of very sweet tea, cheese, soft white bread, and a copper bowl of ripe apricots with freckles on their cheeks.

The very smell of the food at first made the boy feel faint. But he quickly got over that. If he was to live among the Infidels, he reasoned, he would have to eat their food or starve. And he had been hungry a long time. By the time he had finished eating the last crumb of the bread and cheese and polished off three apricots and many cups of hot tea, he was feeling much more at ease with the world.

WHEN CAPTAIN VLASTOV CAME TO RECLAIM HIS CHARGE from the comforts of the staff officers' dining room, the preparations for the long trip north were completed.

"You are leaving this morning?" the lieutenant asked rather incredulously. "You will give the boy no time to rest? Or yourselves?"

"Time is a luxury we lack in this case," said Vlastov. "General Pullo feels it will be to our advantage to have the hostage out of the area before his father is informed. You see, Shamil believes the boy will be held locally. I doubt he will be pleased to learn otherwise."

"But surely now the Murids will surrender?"

Vlastov shook his head. "I doubt that. They have never known when to quit. In any event, our orders are to proceed immediately to Moscow and then to St. Petersburg."

"If you will permit my saying so, sir, I think this trip may be very hard on the boy."

"Yes," agreed Vlastov, "and it will be even harder on Von Cernea and me. I do not look forward with joy to bouncing for a thousand miles in that wretched wagon."

"But at least you will be bouncing in your own time, sir," said the lieutenant, "if you understand my meaning? This boy will be traveling from the twelfth century to the nineteenth."

Vlastov gave the young man a long shrewd look. "You think too much, Lieutenant," he said with a smile. "It is a habit to be avoided in the military." He held out his gloved hand to Jemal-Edin. "Come along now, son," he said, and then again to the lieutenant, "Thank you for seeing that he ate something. He wouldn't eat for us."

Jemal-Edin looked from one face to the other, wishing he could understand what they were saying about him. Automatically he gripped the hilt of his dagger for reassurance and comfort. His gesture did not go unnoticed.

"Who returned that damn knife to him?"

"He will not use it, sir. I have his word as a gentleman."

"You have his word! He understands Russian? French?"

"No, sir. He understands the code of chivalry." As he saw Vlastov hesitating over whether or not to take the dagger from the boy again, the young man said, "It is his only personal possession, sir, and obviously very precious to him."

"Oh all right. I suppose we can take it away from him later if he becomes frisky."

Outside again Jemal-Edin saw that a sturdy wagon hitched to a four-horse team was waiting for them in front of the command post. A band of Terek Cossacks mounted on shaggy, half-wild ponies waited to escort them. He was helped up into the wagon bed to sit on a soft pile of sheepskins; Vlastov and Von Cernea joined him. The driver clucked to the horses, and they began their long journey with no more fanfare than if they had been heading toward the next fort.

The maroon wagon was a buckboardlike affair, seatless, springless, and sturdy. And very uncomfortable. Men and boy alike bounced over every rut and stone. The pile of straw and sheepskins in the wagon helped a little to cushion the jolts, but not very much. But Jemal-Edin was too busy watching the Cossacks riding along beside them to pay attention to the discomfort.

Although he had never really seen them before, he knew what Cossacks were from hearing his father's warriors talk about them. People of the steppes and lowlands to the north, they had long been enemies. Tight-jacketed, pig-tailed hair, short, swarthy, and very muscular, they clung to their ponies like centaurs. They wore baggy black velvet pants smeared with pitch to show their disdain for such fine fabric. The heels of their boots were capped with silver, as were their whip handles. The hilts and sheaths of their other weapons were engraved in gold and silver.

As the wagon creaked out of the garrison town, the Cossacks boiled about it in an undisciplined swarm, riding up close to get a good look at the son of their arch enemy and galloping away as if they did not care after all. Finally Von Cernea shouted a command to their leader, telling him to keep his men behind the wagon. They were causing entirely too much dust!

Jemal-Edin was sorry when the Cossacks fell back; he had enjoyed watching them. They were almost as fine horsemen as the Murids. He looked at the Russian officers who sat disconsolately, braced against either side of the wagon box for back support, their long booted legs forming a fence on either side of him. They were smoking their perpetual cigars and talking, ignoring him. He sighed. It was going to be a long dull ride.

It was a beautiful day, clear and crisp, the unnatural heat wave ended by a northwind. High above them on both sides the jagged peaks glittered with snow against the blue sky, and the waterfalls flashed against the cliffs. As the wagon rumbled along the rutted road, pheasants croaked and quail called, wood thrush and finches sang in the woods around them.

The boy took the great beauty of the country for granted. He had always lived there and knew nothing else. What he thought about now as he watched the Cossacks riding behind was Baba. But that was a bad thing to remember. He forced it out of his mind. Better to think about the Infidels.

He decided it had been silly of him to have been so afraid when Shamil told him he would have to go to them. But then he had always been told all Infidels were monsters, that they made slaves of all captives and marched them off in long lines into endless snow.

But these Infidels were apparently not that way. Perhaps there were different tribes of them?

But why didn't they ride horses like the other men? Was it a mark of honor to be able to endure the torture of these wheeled boxes? Maybe they were testing him? Well, if that were the case, he would show them he could endure the punishment as long as they could. Having made that decision, he arranged the sheepskins beneath him and stretched out upon them, pulled his white woolly hat down so that it shielded his eyes against the sun's glare, and promptly fell asleep.

Near twilight they came to a large fort and stopped only long enough to eat while a fresh team was hitched to the wagon. Here, as everywhere else they would stop on the long journey, the boy found himself an object of great curiosity among both officers and men. All wanted to see the son of Shamil, and their interest made him both proud and ill at ease.

Von Cernea and Vlastov kept him close beside them at all times. Many Russian or Cossack soldiers whose friends or brothers had died horribly in Shamil's prison pits would have felt it worth the price of instant death to kill the son of Shamil. Nor was it only Russian troops who had this great hatred for Shamil. For in his efforts to unite the Caucasus against foreign conquest, where oratory or faith had failed to convert tribes to his way of thinking, Shamil had too often had his Murids ruthlessly kill entire families as an example of what happened to those who defied him. This mercilessness had created for him some bitter and powerful enemies, one of whom was the autocratic sultan who had spoken to Jemal-Edin at Temir-Khan-Shura. Added to these dangers was the chance of rampaging Murids who had never reached Ak-hulgo suddenly riding down out of the forest, hoping to curry favor with their Imam by rescuing and re-turning his son.

Jemal-Edin noticed the two officers seemed much relieved when finally, after several days and nights on the road, the wagon and its Cossack escort were out of that part of the mountains with which he was fa-miliar. The trip grew more interesting to him now. The wagon bumped along beside a rushing river, wider and deeper than any he had ever seen before. The taller of the two officers pointed to it and said "Terek" several times.

Under the looming grandeur of immense moun-tains, they stopped at another fort to change teams again. This was an old established base; the walls of the fort were stone topped by heavy spiked timbers. It stood on a hill up away from the river, its gate facing north, toward the Darial Gorge.

As the exhausted teams were led away for rest and pasture before being returned to their home fort, four fresh horses were brought out by the military grooms. Jemal-Edin looked at them in amazement. He had never seen horses so large; they had legs like logs and hoofs like his mother's rice pot! In a second he was out the door of the officers' mess and standing beside the red wagon, watching with great interest.

"Can they run, those horses?" he asked the young groom in his outlandish tongue. The groom, trying to back the first team over the double-tree to hitch them, glanced at the boy in his white suit just in time to see him squat down and try to touch the huge hoof of the horse nearest to him.

"Keep back! They'll kick your silly head off!"

Jemal-Edin obeyed, looking a bit sheepish. The language did not matter; the tone was clear. He had been around horses too long not to know he had just done a very foolish thing. The big horses snorted and stamped at the strange scent of him. Their massive iron shoes left deep imprints in the packed earth of the stableyard. For a moment Jemal-Edin stared at the groom's angry and frightened face, and then he bowed in silent apology to the boy who was only a few years older than himself. The groom gave him a lopsided grin. There were running footsteps behind them. He turned to see the taller captain come hurrying from his meal, his napkin still in hand.

"So this is what made you run off," Vlastov said as Jemal-Edin pointed at the huge horses to share his wonder. "You have never seen dray horses, have you? I admit they are quite different from your father's stallions. But they will get us where we must go." Then, turning to Von Cernea who had come out to see if everything was all right, he added, "Dear God, Kurt, we're beginning to act like a pair of worried nannies!"

The teams were hitched without further incident but with Jemal-Edin watching the whole operation closely. When the entourage left the fort, he was sitting beside the driver, marveling at the broad rear ends of the powerful horses as they clomped slowly down the hill and back onto the Georgian Military Highway.

This road, built at great expense and waste of lives, was another wonder to Jemal-Edin. He had never seen a real road before. It followed the Terek River through the gorge, sometimes running along beside the water, sometimes climbing the adjoining cliffs. Then it left the river and wound around the peaks, clinging to cliffs wherever it could, up and up until even these huge horses were straining every muscle to pull the wagon.

There, on top of the pass, stood a huge cross like a T against the sky. Seeing it, Jemal-Edin spat over the side of the wagon to avert the evil eye, and looked away from this symbol of the Infidel. As they began to descend, on distant cliffs he saw the ruins of ancient castles and wondered what fortresses these had been and when they had fallen.

The wooden brakes on the rear wheels of the wagon became so hot from constant application that he could smell them burning and saw they were beginning to smoke. He watched Von Cernea, who had sat very quietly all afternoon, turn a little green as he looked out over the edge of the wagon and saw nothing but air and the river far below. Although it was windy and very cold up here on the heights, the man was sweating. He tugged at his collar for a moment, then shifted carefully to the other side of the wagon against the cliff face. They rounded a curve in the roadway. Ahead of them the advance Cossacks had dismounted and were clearing the road of a small avalanche of boulders and earth.

"Are we to be trapped on this eagle's aerie?" Von Cernea asked nervously. "My stomach has never adjusted fully to these altitudes."

"This is a minor delay," Vlastov assured him. "You should take this road by ox cart after an early snowfall. That would provide thrills you would never forget!"

"I think I will get out and walk for a little way," the other officer said. "I refuse even to think about the pass with snow on it." He held out his hand in invitation for the boy to join him as the wagon came to a halt. Jemal-Edin took the proffered hand for the first time without thinking that he was enduring the disgusting touch of an unbeliever.

Man and boy stood for a time, watching the guards clear the roadbed. Although he was bored, Jemal-Edin made no effort to help. An Avar noble left all manual labor to other men; if he did not have slaves, he hired lesser men to handle such matters.

At the end of the pass, they came upon a supply wagon train waiting for them to clear the route before it could proceed upward on its way to Tiflis in Georgia. The horses were changed again at a Cossack fort at nightfall and they continued on into the foothills. Here the escort of Terek River Cossacks was replaced by a troop from the Don.

IN THE FOOTHILLS, WITH SNOW-CAPPED PEAKS AS A backdrop, lay the town of Vladikavkaz, a trading post on the ancient route to the Georgian south. Horse and camel traders came here from provinces far to the east. Along the dusty streets beneath the flowering acacias bulgy-kneed Bactrian camels plodded, their half-closed aristocratic eyes and sneering lips showing the scorn with which they regarded not only the warm weather and their present employment as pack animals, but everything and everyone about them.

Jemal-Edin had never seen Bactrian camels before and they pleased him very much. He was delighted when they groaned and spat and flicked their skins to set the camel bells ajingle. Even more interesting to him was the vast horse market where, among the nondescript Russian and Cossack breeds, were the beautiful and very expensive horses from the khanate of Kabarda. These horses the Murids prized above all others and they had on several occasions raided this very market to obtain them.

There was a bank, a post office and a courthouse which Jemal-Edin, who had never seen a town before, thought were large houses. There was a mosque and an onion-domed Russian Orthodox cathedral, restaurants, inns, and steambaths. Along the river was a park with a white wooden bandstand, flower gardens, and a fountain. In the vast bazaar rug merchants displayed the rich and exotic weavings of the nomad and mountain tribes. There were strange meats, fruits and vegetables, Persian silks, spices, saddles, silver and ivory, guns and sabers, and samovars of gleaming brass.

It was almost too much for Jemal-Edin to take in during his brief ride through the town. Especially since his view was blocked much of the time by the Cossack guards who surrounded the wagon to prevent a possible assassination attempt on their hostage. Only when the wagon had left the town and green fields lined the road, did the guard detail move away.

In the fields along the road farmers were plowing with water buffalo. These too were new to the mountain boy and he stared at them in wonder. That such huge beasts with their obviously powerful horns could be made to do such demeaning work amazed him.

The road ended. They did not reach another for over five hundred miles. They traveled through the vast marshes of the Don, then into open steppe country, grassland marked only by the dim ruts made by caravans. They passed several of these daily, merchants and army supply trains heading south before winter could overtake them with heavily loaded wagons, pack trains, and cart after cart pulled by slow-moving oxen.

The steppes were dry, their coarse grass covered with dust. The land was frightening to Jemal-Edin. Having always lived hemmed in by mountains, he thought nothing else existed. This huge open space, this emptiness, made him feel exposed and uneasy.

Afterwards he remembered always two things he had seen on the steppes. One was a herd of saiga antelope. He did not know what they were then, only that they were the strangest-looking animals he had ever seen. The size of a large sheep, they had long spindly legs and shabby fur. But unlike sheep, their faces ended in a nose so long that it hung down over their mouths and dangled as they ran. And run they did! By almost limitless thousands the herd enveloped and swirled around the wagon and outriders. To keep the horses from bolting in fear, the Cossacks and both captains shot constantly until a fence of dead saiga protected them from the masses of the living. It took more than an hour for the herd to pass by and half the afternoon for the dust left in their wake to settle.

The other thing that impressed Jemal-Edin was an endless line of man-made mounds stretching over the open steppe where no man lived. Atop each mound was a stone image of a woman. The women were round-cheeked, their breasts bare. They stood slope-shouldered with hands folded over what appeared to be a box or book. On their heads they wore hats like a fez with veils down their backs. Their lips were narrow and their stone eyes looked out with haunting patience across the emptiness that surrounded them.

They gave Jemal-Edin no feeling of evil as the Infidel cross had, but only a sense of great age and mystery. He wanted to stop and look at them. The captains, of course, did not understand his request. But when the Cossacks shot at the images for sport, Jemal-Edin shouted at them in outraged anger until finally Vlastov ordered the men to quit firing.

Sometimes the travelers would come upon one of the decrepit inns scattered along the common route and then Jemal-Edin would marvel at the wonders of civilization. Aside from the brass brazierlike mosque lamps, he had never seen a lamp or lantern before, and found them marvelous things. That one could have a light at night pleased him very much. He resolved to bring one of these beautiful and useful things home to his mother so that she might enjoy it. He decided that these wretched innkeepers must be great khans, so wealthy that they could afford to waste oil this way, and use cloth to cover their tables. Yet they bowed and cowered and showed great deference to his captains.

Isolated as he was by age and the language and cultural barriers, though good-naturedly cared for physically by the two officers, Jemal-Edin was for the most part ignored by them. He was a duty which they had to dispatch. Nothing more. While they rested from the wagon ride by playing cards and drinking with other officers encountered at the inns, he was left to fall asleep at the table or curl up next to the huge tile stove until it was time again to get into the red wagon and hurry on to the north. The loneliness he had felt among his own people was mild compared to what he knew now.

The towns became more frequent in the northern Ukraine. Many-domed churches appeared on the grassy horizons. Then came the birch forests—and rain. Mile after mile of cold gray rain turned the trip into sheer misery. The horses slogged along, their hoofs, like the wagon's wheels, throwing daubs of mud. The captains and Cossacks were enveloped in oilskins and moroseness.

Jemal-Edin pulled his cloak up over his hat and sat hunched upon the wet straw as if in a small tent. He was too cold and too tired out to sleep much of the time. He passed the hours trying without success not to think about home. He had been right, he decided, they would never let him go back. He was too far away now ever to return. He wondered if Shamil had known he would be taken so far, so many jolts and bounces and days of lonely silence away.

The rain finally stopped. They reached a recognizable road once more. The passing days were shorter and cooler. He wore his long cloak all the time. The words the captains said to him as they entered each new town made little sense. First there had been Rostov, then after the saiga came Kharkov. In the rain they passed through Orel and then Tula. He had nodded at each name and stored it away to consider later when he felt better. He barely looked at the towns now. The final weeks of Akhulgo's siege and starvation followed by this endless trip were beginning to tell on him. He could hardly get in and out of the wagon without help. It took all his pride and strength just to keep the men from knowing how exhausted he was.

And then one evening, three weeks after leaving Akhulgo, the red wagon rumbled into Moscow. He had been asleep, and the new noise of the iron wheels on the cobbled streets woke him. He sat up and his mouth fell open. The sun was going down and its last rays set aflame the golden domes of St. Basils, glittered off the strange double-headed eagle atop the Kremlin gate, and turned the windows of each building to reddish-pink fire.

There was too much to see all at once! He turned this way and that in the wagon, trying to take it all in, trying not to be scared. There were so many buildings, so many people, so many horses and vans, so many noises, enormous coaches with liveried coachmen, vendors hawking food on street corners, bright uniforms, bright-colored clothing—and women unveiled and walking the streets openly!

As they drove on into the center of the city the houses became lit from within. He could see fabric draping the windows and people moving about inside. In some of the streets he saw torches on top of poles, fires encased in glass to light the night. There were so many things he wanted to ask about and he burned with curiosity. But there was no one with whom he could discuss it.

They stopped at last in front of a huge red palace, the residence of the governor general of Moscow. The captains climbed down from the wagon and helped him down. The Cossack escort rode through an iron gate to disappear into a stableyard.

Jemal-Edin, mouth still open, stood at the foot of a long sweep of marble steps leading to the door. The driver of the wagon spoke to the horses and the wagon moved off, out of the boy's life.

Above him the captains smiled to each other at his awe of this city and then led him into the building. Inside the main hall, an enormous yellow chandelier hung over a flight of steps winding up to the offices of the governor general. Its crystals sparkled and twinkled in the candlelight. Jemal-Edin thought it the most beautiful thing he had ever seen. Instantly he made up his mind that, if ever he were allowed to leave the Infidels, this was the sort of lamp he would take to his mother, not the common lanterns of the inns. He stumbled twice going up the stairs from looking back over his shoulder at the chandelier hanging overhead.

He listened in the governor general's office while the men talked, wondering if this were the Great White Sultan. Again there was no interpreter who spoke his language, and besides, the governor general had little time for the minor business of a hostage. It was good that the men were there, of course.

"You gentlemen will, undoubtedly, wish to dine with your regimental brothers tonight," he said to Captains Vlastov and Von Cernea. "Give you a small interlude from guard duty. I will have my secretary take care of the boy." He called to an aide who in turn fetched another man.

Understanding only that he was to accompany this

new stranger, Jemal-Edin did so. He was taken down a long carpeted marble hallway and given into the care of another stranger. This second stranger attempted to speak with him, and learning he could not communicate, called to still another man. Finally an old woman with a white cloth about her ample waist and another tied over her gray hair appeared and led the boy to a servants' kitchen.

There he was given strange food, and when he had eaten, the old woman took him to a small dark room and put him to bed in a comforter on the floor. Like a trapped wild thing that seeks escape from reality, he fell asleep almost instantly.

Before sunrise, they were on their way to St. Petersburg, traveling by fast carriage over the one good road in all Russia. This road was relatively flat and kept in some repair because, as Von Cernea told Vlastov, "It is the only road Czar Nicholas regularly travels."

ALMOST THE ONLY SOUND TO BREAK THE SILENCE AS THE
czar impatiently flipped through the pages of dis-
patches the captain had carried was the rustle of the
paper itself. Flanked by his captains, Jemal-Edin
stood at attention some distance from the desk behind
which Nicholas I sat reading with obvious displeasure.

Both the czar and his palace were very different
from what Jemal-Edin had expected. After the stories
he had been told all his life, he had pictured the
Great White Sultan as a fearsome giant dressed in
flowing white robes and a huge turban; a creature
breathing fire and smoke, stalking his shadowed
djinn's cave with a whip in one hand and a curved
saber in the other, crushing the bones of the unfortunate beneath his feet as he went—or perhaps pausing
now and then in his murderous rages to run his hands
through glowing piles of polished gems or sensuously

caress gleaming vessels of gold and silver. On ledges about the cave would be stretched languorous veiled beauties, like houris in the Persian myths, while cringing slaves skulked and fawned before the sultan's might.

For three weeks, ever since the sultan at the garrison town had told him he was to be sent north to meet the czar, Jemal-Edin had looked forward to this hour with growing dread. So it had been a great shock, if not a pleasant surprise, when he was escorted into the czar's office and, after looking about for someone resembling the giant he imagined, realized by the attitudes of the men around him that they served the tall man behind the desk. An ordinary man! A man who looked like other men, if more grandly dressed. After the first surge of relief had passed, Jemal-Edin found there was something familiar about the man—he reminded him of his father, Shamil.

It was an accurate impression. Physically and mentally the two rulers had much in common. Both were very tall and slender, both immaculate in dress and grooming. Both had eyes that glared with insane rage at the slightest hint of displeasure. Both truly believed they ruled at the direct wish of their respective God—and anyone rash enough to question their wishes questioned God Himself. Both loved war, although Shamil was a true warrior, whereas Nicholas I loved the idea of war but found actual battles extremely untidy. Both possessed the power and ruthlessness to be cruel beyond imagination. Both could be extraordinarily kind and sentimental at unexpected moments. And both loved and were loved by children who perhaps recognized in these awful men the child that never had to grow up.

Jemal-Edin knew the sultan was angry because he had often seen the same look on his father's face. The expression on the faces of the other men in the office was also familiar, a mixture of apprehension, awe, respect, and fear. But the boy was accustomed to tyrants, and at the moment he was far more interested in looking about the room, admiring the lush green fabric on the walls. Green was the color of the Prophet and greatly favored by warriors. Through the windows behind the sultan he could see the walls and top of a great fortress, and wondered if it were the same building he had seen from the carriage earlier that day.

As the silence continued his mind wandered, seeing again the second of the great cities of the Infidels to which he had been brought. Truly had the sultan in the green uniform called them great! He, Jemal-Edin, could never have imagined that men could build anything so large or so wondrous as these cities! Twice as they drove into St. Petersburg the officers had had to grab him to keep him from falling out of the carriage. He had stood up on the seat in order to have a better view of the broad streets, the enormous churches, the canals and bridges, the river wider than a sea and forced to flow between banks of marble, the boats which sailed upon it. He had never seen a boat before.

There were palaces of yellow, blue, red, violet, and all were enormous. The largest palace of all was the maroon Winter Palace housing the office in which they now stood. Although he knew the name for none of this, he could tell by the size and grandeur of the place that this was the end of his journey.

It was very clear to him that the White Sultan, or the czar as they called him here, was a vastly more powerful ruler than Shamil. It had taken only three days to cross the land Shamil ruled; but three weeks to cross the czar's kingdom. And all of the Avar tribe plus all the other tribes of the Caucasus could not have filled this city. But one thing above all else made the difference in power apparent to him—the size and magnificence of this house in which the White Sultan lived!

Shamil's finest house was a two-story affair of stucco and stone. It contained six rooms and three small windows of precious glass. Aside from the housekeeping implements, the pots and pans, it was furnished only with pillows, rugs, and felt mats. The only stairs was outside, a series of notches cut into the rock leading to the second floor. As he looked about the office Jemal-Edin decided that the whole house could have been tucked into this one room with space to spare.

As this realization occurred to him, the boy wondered if his father truly understood the power of the enemy he defied.

The boy studied the man behind the desk. He was tall and stern as a leader of men should be, and richly dressed in a white uniform trimmed with gold braid and sable. As though aware he was being watched, the great sultan looked up from his papers, his pale blue eyes narrowing to focus on the boy. Beside him,

Jemal-Edin felt Vlastov shift slightly in unease and he glanced up at him. When he looked again at the czar, the man had returned to his reading.

Nicholas threw down the papers in disgust. "They contain little that is new, gentlemen," he said shortly, "nothing that pleases me, and much that has since been undone. Were you aware that the hostage's father, a most troublesome man, along with a wife, a young son, and several henchmen, escaped from that crag? That, after costing us half our army, we have let that pirate turn our glorious victory to ashes? No! I can tell by the vacuous looks on your faces you were in ignorance of that information. Ignorance seems to be the normal state for my officers."

He rose from his chair and circled the desk to stand directly in front of them. The men stiffened still more at attention. Behind his back his secretary, aides, and staff officers relaxed slightly. The czar waved in the direction of Jemal-Edin. "This is the hostage? This is the 'Lion's' cub?"

"Yes, Your Majesty."

"Did he give you any trouble? Or are my officers competent when it comes to dealing with small boys?"

"He is well behaved, Your Majesty," Vlastov said nervously.

"He is also dusty as a gutter sparrow!" the czar snapped. "You, gentlemen, reek of cologne, bath-water, and the pressing cloth. But this boy, if I am correct, has not had a change of clothing since leaving his home?"

"We had no other uniform for him, Your Majesty," Von Cernea said apologetically.

"Was it also impossible to find someone to bathe him and brush his garments?"

The words were a mystery but the threat they contained was not. The brutally cold sarcasm in the czar's voice made Jemal-Edin shiver. When his father used this tone of voice to his men, the scene usually ended in violence. He looked up at the Great Sultan, his grave brown eyes very large and pleading. He bowed as the young lieutenant had shown him.

"Your warriors have been good to me," he told the sultan in Arabic, hoping against hope that he could be understood by someone in the room. "They have shown me only honor and kindness. If by doing so they have displeased you, Oh Mighty One, I beg you for their lives. My father, the Imam Shamil, entrusted me to their care."

"What does he say?" the czar demanded.

From the corner of the big office a court interpreter stepped forward, bowed, and then translated the Arabic to Russian. The czar stared unblinkingly at Jemal-Edin during the entire time the translator spoke. Jemal-Edin returned the gaze without flinching. Then the czar smiled slightly. Jemal-Edin smiled back at him.

"What an extraordinarily sweet smile the boy has," Nicholas commented to no one in particular. "He is charming! One would never guess him to be sired by a rebel. I am told he is of noble blood. Is that correct?"

"So it is said, Your Majesty."

"Yes," the czar nodded with satisfaction at his own insight. "Blood always tells! The boy is obviously an aristocrat. He will make a fine officer in my army. And he has the gift of gratitude—even to two men who have left him to rot in his clothes for nearly a month. Mahmet," he inclined his head to the interpreter, "inform the boy I am ordering these officers to return to the Caucasus. Now! And due to his gracious intercession on their behalf, I am promoting them both to colonel."

As the translator explained the czar's command, Jemal-Edin saw the captains salute the czar and bow in gratitude for his imperial clemency. Then, with a sinking feeling, he saw they had been dismissed and were leaving the room—leaving him. They were the enemy, but they had been kind to him in their way. And they were his last link with home. He wanted to run after them, beg them to take him along with them. But that would be unseemly. He must be brave. He watched the ornately gilded doors shut behind them and clenched his fists for self-control. Then, remembering in whose presence he stood, he turned again at stiff attention to face the czar.

Nicholas was watching him thoughtfully, his blond mustache moving as he absent-mindedly chewed the corner of his upper lip. He turned and walked back to his chair behind the desk.

"Tell the boy to come here and sit beside me," he commanded. Jemal-Edin did as he was told, sinking with relief to the carpet in front of the czar's chair and folding his legs beneath him, Avar fashion.

"It is much too drafty to sit on the floor, child. Tell him to sit on that chair. Bring it up here, closer to me."

Jemal-Edin had never sat in a chair before. This one, designed for the long-legged czar's comfort, he found quite awkward. The seat was too far off the ground, and his legs swung until he thought of tucking them beneath him. The White Sultan watched patiently until his guest was comfortably settled. Jemal-Edin took it for granted that this man, who could be an ogre to his men and to his whole people, could be gentle and considerate of him. Shamil had taught his son that a true warrior was gentle to women, children, and pets; there was no honor in unnecessarily hurting the defenseless.

"I want you to know, Jemal-Edin," Nicholas said through the interpreter, "that I myself and all my generals have great respect and admiration for your father. It is unfortunate that we are on opposing sides in this war. I would be greatly honored to have such a fine strategist as one of my officers."

The boy gravely watched the blond man's face as the czar spoke, seeking to know both his fate and the sincerity of the man's words. Avar speech was far more flowery than this, far more elaborate. Had it been Shamil speaking in this situation, Jemal-Edin knew his father would have spent at least an hour gracefully extolling the virtues of his enemy to his enemy's son. It was only polite to do so by Avar custom. For the greater the esteem and power of the enemy, the greater the honor in capturing his son and in eventually defeating the father. And after such warmth and sincere praise, if Shamil deemed it politic, he would order the son whipped and thrown down into a prison pit with starved rats and giant sheep ticks for company, or, if he wished to show mercy, put to death.

Now Jemal-Edin heard his father dismissed in three sentences. Apparently this man had little real regard or respect for Shamil. Or was he being shrewd and concealing that respect from the son? Jemal-Edin could not be sure, and his thoughts were interrupted by the translator who was speaking again.

"You are, of course, a hostage. But being a hostage need not be unpleasant. The duration of your visit depends upon your father. It may be quite long. I am told he is a very stubborn man. However, I will give you every opportunity to benefit by your stay with us, to go to school, to learn all you can of the world and all it has to offer. In a short time, when you are more familiar with us and with our customs and language, I want you to enter the Corps des Pages so that you may serve me here in the palace and live here where I may watch over you personally." Nicholas paused and smiled while Mahmet translated this to Jemal-Edin, who soberly nodded his understanding, if not his belief.

"Do you miss your family very much?" Nicholas wanted to know.

The boy nodded again, not trusting himself to speak for a moment. He was unprepared by the bluntness of the question. An Avar would not ask such a personal question under these circumstances. He had tried not to think of his family or what had become of them, and the reminder of them brought tears of pain to his eyes. But rather than make the unmanly admission that he was very worried about his mother and little brother in particular, he said, "I miss my horse. He was such a good horse. His name was Baba. I had to hide him from the Infidel. It is said they eat horses . . ."

"That is not true!" lied the czar. "Never believe that! My men would not do such a thing! And to replace your loss, I will give you a horse. You may have your pick of any horse in my stable. I will have my son, the Grand Duke Constantine, accompany you to my stables tomorrow. He is about your age. I am sure you will like each other. He spends half his time in the stable—when we can get him away from his books. I am sure he can tell you which of the horses is the best. But then, of course, you are an experienced horseman and you will know which animal to choose."

It was impossible for Jemal-Edin to misinterpret the genuine kindness and concern in the czar's tone of voice and as he heard the translation from Mahmet, the boy turned his face away from the man until he could regain his self-control. An Avar does not cry.

After almost a month of being intermittently frightened, ignored, handled by strange Infidels, exposed to new and very puzzling things and experiences, he was exhausted. He knew his expression should be blank, but he could no longer trust himself. For all that time he had waited and expected to be taken into the presence of an individual who would surely want bloody vengeance against the son of his great enemy. And then to find this man was apparently going to be both gracious and good to him! It was almost more than he could accept and he twisted in discomfort on the silk-covered chair.

"This poor child has blue rings of exhaustion around his eyes, and we keep him here talking," the czar said aloud, disregarding the fact that only *he* was guilty of that charge. "What he needs now more than anything else is a nanny. Son, the major here is my aide-de-camp. He will take you to the home of one of my courtiers where you will live with the other children. They are expecting you and will be most happy to see you have arrived. When you have had time to rest, then will you come to see me again?"

"Yes, sir." Jemal-Edin promised as he unfolded his legs and slid down off the chair. It struck him that this man treated him as if he were Kazi Mohammed's age, but he was tired and he rather liked the attention. He had almost decided he liked the Great Sultan in spite of what he had always been told about him.

"And remember, the Grand Duke will call for you tomorrow and go with you to the Imperial Stables. I want you to have a horse of your own."

"Yes, sir. Thank you very much."

"It has been my pleasure," the czar said with great sincerity. He saluted the boy, who hesitated for a moment, then returned a good imitation of the salute before following the major from the office. The czar permitted himself another slight smile.

"Mahmet," he commanded, "go with the boy. Stay with him until he has learned enough Russian to communicate. He has already spent too long a time in silence."

Jemal-Edin was so tired that he remembered little of his first night in the home of Feodor Shchukin. He was met at the door by a man in pale-yellow livery who was soon joined by a very beautiful lady who made a great and very comforting fuss, welcoming him and saying that he would be her adopted son. She called in a round-faced young woman with rosy cheeks who took him upstairs, removed his filthy white clothing, and bathed him in a huge copper tub. After his bath, she brought his dinner, and then put him to bed in a nursery where two other children of the household were already asleep.

When she had tucked him in and left, taking the lamp with her, the only light in the room was a candle flickering in a red glass in front of the icon on the bureau. Jemal-Edin sighed and relaxed for the first time in many days.

As he stretched out under the soft comforter and stared at the candle flame, his eyelids began to drop. He was asleep and dreaming, seeing again the flickering flames of Akhulgo, the savagery, the killing, remembering the smell of death. He heard the women wailing, the dusty whisk of the vultures' wings. His mother was crying, and his brother was running along the cliff, calling out to him. Shamil was there in black with outstretched arms that became the wings of a vulture tipped with blue flame. He wanted to run, run away from them all, from the flames and the killing and the horror . . . but his legs were heavy and he could only crawl. It was coming after him! The horror was going to catch him!

"Shhhh . . . shhhh . . ." The nanny was sitting on the edge of his bed, cuddling him against her softness and warmth and safety. He threw his arms around her neck and shuddered, remembering the nightmare and wanting more than anything else to forget it, forget it all as she rocked him and crooned to him in the universal language of comfort.

But for many nights thereafter the dream would return and he would be there again, in Akhulgo, trapped into the terror of the past.

"LOOK, FEO, HE HAS VERY LONG EYELASHES. AND HIS hair is more curly than yours. I think he is beautiful!"

"Men are not beautiful. Men are handsome. And it is not polite to watch someone when they are sleeping."

The buzzing whisper of the conversation beside his bed seeped through Jemal-Edin's mind. He opened his eyes with a start, then closed them against the glare of sunlight that streamed through the windows of the cheerful nursery.

"See. Now you have wakened him. Mama said he was to be let sleep for as long as he could this morning."

"But if he is to be our new brother, I want to meet him!"

Jemal-Edin opened his eyes again, more cautiously this time. The first person he saw was Mahmet slumped in a chair by the stove. To the right of his bed stood a dark-haired boy about his own age dressed in blue. Next to him, a little girl with thick blond curls. She was wearing a white dress with puffed sleeves and a blue silk sash, a dress so short her chubby knees showed above her white stockings and black shoes. She was, he decided, the prettiest little girl he had ever seen. He sat up in bed, pulling the covers around himself since he could not recall if he was dressed or not.

"Good morning," the little girl said in French. She curtsied.

"Good morning." The boy stepped forward with a formal bow. "I am Feodor Feodorovitch Shchukin. This is my sister, Sophia Tatiana Feodorovna. We welcome you to our home, and hope that you will enjoy living here."

Jemal-Edin's serious gaze fastened first on one, then the other, then looked over at Mahmet for help. Mahmet got to his feet resignedly, his face saying plainly that he felt his present post somewhat beneath his skills. "The boy says his name is Feodor but they call him Feo. The girl is Sophia. They welcome you to their home and wish you well."

Through Mahmet, Jemal-Edin introduced himself and thanked them for their welcome. Brother and sister began to talk at once, and Mahmet was kept busy translating while Jemal-Edin struggled to absorb all the two said.

Sophia wanted to know if he liked being in St. Petersburg, and did he like to ice skate, and when he was dressed would he come and look at her toys? Feo, being more mature, informed him that he was very welcome to share his wardrobe until the tailor had been called, and new clothing prepared for Jemal-Edin. And they would share the same tutor whose name was André, who was French and rather nice. And might he look at Jemal-Edin's dagger which he had seen Nanny put away on top of the bookcase the night before?

Mahmet was bringing down the dagger and belt when Nanny came into the room. "No!" she said automatically, shaking her head to reinforce the meaning, and then seeing the look on the boy's face, hesitated. She took the knife from Mahmet and handed it to Jemal-Edin who hugged it against the chest of his nightshirt.

Nanny sat down on the edge of the bed and looked from the Shchukin children to Jemal-Edin and back again, torn between what she felt to be an obvious danger to children and depriving one of them of something he apparently treasured. "Is it so precious to him?" she asked Mahmet in Russian.

"I think so, miss," said the man, who was a Georgian. "In the high country they are given their daggers in the cradle as you would give a baby a rattle. Before they can lisp their first words, they know how to use it. Why I have seen children of ten who had already killed . . . but that is not for the ears of these children."

"We have been told that he is to forget all that, forget the past," she said and then, turning her attention to Feo and Sophia. "We shall need your help, your mother and father and I. Jemal-Edin has had a very sad life. Now that he is here, you can help him forget the bad things that have happened to him. I want you to promise me that you will not ask him about his mother and father or how he came here, or talk to him about war. And if he talks about it, you are to change the subject. Will you promise me that?"

"What happened to him?" Sophia wanted to know.

"That does not matter now. What is important is that it is over and he is here with us and needs our help very much."

"Is that why he does not smile?" asked Feo.

"Yes, I think so. Will you promise me?"

"Yes, Nanny," said Feo very seriously.

"Me, too," said Sophia. "You stay here. I am going to get him something that will make him happy." She scooted out of the big room, her patent leather shoes flashing as she ran.

Nanny turned her attention to the sober Jemal-Edin. "In this household, Jemal-Edin," she began haltingly, ". . . it is not the custom for boys and girls to wear weapons. There is no need for them. There are no enemies here. Because the children are unused to weapons such as your beautiful dagger, it worries me that Sophia or one of the babies might find it. They might think it a toy and badly injure themselves with it."

"He will not know what a toy is, miss," Mahmet interjected before translating. The young woman stared at him, then shook her head ruefully.

"Tell him he may always keep his dagger, but that I wish he would not wear it about the house. That if he permits it, I will put it where only he may know where it is hidden."

Jemal-Edin listened to these words, then shook his head, no!

"I will wear it," he insisted. "If I wear it, no one else can touch it. I will not use it. I have my honor. But I will wear it!"

Upon hearing his reply Nanny shook her head in resignation. Her instructions were not to upset the boy any more than he had been upset. And since he was in the household at the express wishes of the emperor, those instructions had to be obeyed. But . . .

"If you should change your mind," she said, "will you trust me to keep the dagger for you?"

"I will wear it!" Jemal-Edin insisted.

There was a clatter of running footsteps in the hall outside. "Look what I have for you!" Sophia shouted as she burst in the door. Clutched to her chest was a fat floppy-eared puppy who was whimpering from being juggled so rapidly as his mistress ran up the steps. "It's the prettiest one of the litter, and I want you to have it!" she announced to the boy as she triumphantly deposited the frightened little animal on the covers in front of him.

Jemal-Edin looked down at the curly-haired fur ball, then back at Sophia. It was obviously a dog, but so fat and clean—unlike any he had ever seen. The sheathed dagger and belt slipped unnoticed by him onto the covers.

"She has given you the little dog as a gift," Mahmet told him.

Jemal-Edin's face went very red, and he slowly

reached out and gathered the little dog closer to him. The puppy licked his chin and snuggled against the still warm covers next to the boy.

"What are you going to name it?" demanded Sophia.

"Is it a boy or a girl?"

"I believe it is a girl," said Mahmet.

Jemal-Edin thought for a moment, stroking the silken head. "Then I will call her Saidia. It is a soft gentle name, like the animal. I thank you very much for the gift," he told Sophia. He was going to apologize for not having a gift to give her in return but she interrupted.

"You see! I told you it would make him smile!" she crowed. "I'm hungry, Nanny."

"I will ring for our breakfast. Feodor, will you be good enough to show Jemal-Edin the dressing room and toilet chamber? I think he can manage with the clothing I laid out, but perhaps he will need your help. Come, Sophia, we will go comb your hair while the boys are getting ready for breakfast."

When the boys returned, Jemal-Edin was dressed in the same blue blouselike shirt and tight pants as Feo wore. They found Sophia alone in the nursery. She was sitting on Jemal-Edin's bed, the puppy flopped in sleep against her back—and she was playing with the dagger.

Instinctively Jemal-Edin reached out and stopped Feo from advancing. The Avar boy watched in surprised horror as the little girl grasped the sheath in her left hand and tugged the long knife out. As it pulled free of the sheath the sharp point dipped toward her upturned knee. Careless of the sharp edges, she turned the knife in the sunlight, smiling to see it flash, then brought it up to her face so that she might examine the engraving on the hilt more closely. It had never occured to Jemal-Edin that anyone would handle a dangerous weapon in this manner.

He walked towards her with feigned calm and, as she turned to greet him, held out his hand for the weapon.

"Oh. You want it back, I suppose," she said. "It's very pretty. What does the writing on the shiny part say? It is writing, isn't it?"

She handed the dagger to him pointed end first. He took it between respectful fingertips, reached over for the sheath and slid the knife inside. Then, as he began to belt it over his blouse, he caught Feo's eye and for a moment the two boys looked at each other. Then Jemal-Edin shook his head. This would not do. These people plainly did not know the ways of warriors. He took off the belt and went into the next room where Nanny was talking to Mahmet and silently handed her his dagger.

"Are you sure?" she asked as she took it.

He nodded.

"I am glad. We will put it up here, where no one else can see it and no baby can climb," she said putting it behind the ornate curves atop an armoire. "Whenever you want it, you ask me. Is that acceptable to you?"

He nodded agreement.

"What made you change your mind?"

But he would not say.

At a little after two that afternoon there was a commotion in the street outside the big house and the children rushed to the windows to look out. Before their door stood an enormous coach pulled by eight black horses. Coachmen and lackeys, footmen and guards swarmed about its enameled magnificence. A coachman in brilliant uniform stepped forward to open the huge bayed door bearing the royal coat of arms. A footman bent to let down the coach steps. And from the depths of this enormous conveyance there emerged one small rather homely boy dressed in military uniform. Preceded by two guards and followed by two others, he advanced up the steps of the Shchukin home.

"His Imperial Highness, the Grand Duke Constantine," the butler intoned to Jemal-Edin's baffled ears, "wishes you to be his guest, along with Feodor Feodorovitch, and accompany him on a visit to the Imperial Stables for the purpose of accepting a gift, a horse of the Imperial Stables."

Jemal-Edin saw that Feo was well acquainted with this visitor as he hurried forward and bowed, then shook hands, and brought the boy over to meet the newcomer. Now he understood why he had to change clothes again, this time to riding pants with a coat whose collar nearly choked him. He supposed this was the son of the White Sultan but he was not sure.

He got into the great coach nervously and stared out of its glass windows at the crowd of curious who had gathered at a respectful distance along the street.

The building in front of which they eventually stopped looked so much like a palace that he was astonished to get inside and find it housed only horses.

The stalls were made of highly polished wood with floors of oak blocks bedded over with deep sawdust and straw. In the stalls were horses of every size and description, beautifully kept animals, each one looking finer than the last. Delighted by them all, Jemal-Edin loitered along behind the rather large retinue following the Grand Duke, pausing long in front of each stall to savor the occupant. The Grand Duke stopped before a beautiful black stallion and waited for his guest to join him.

"The czaravitch says that this is the finest stallion in the stables," related Mahmet when Jemal-Edin caught up with the party. "It is from the Orlov stables, and is the horse he would choose if his father allowed him to do so."

Jemal-Edin nodded his understanding and looked at the animal. It was truly fine—but too big, much too big!

"I would have to stand on a rock to get on and off," he told Mahmet. What he did not say was that the black stallion reminded him too much of Shamil's favorite mount. Then, four stalls down, he caught sight of a cream-colored horse. He left the others and ran ahead. Since no one preceded a member of the royal family, this breach of protocol caused a few murmurs from the entourage surrounding the Grand Duke, but Jemal-Edin was unaware of that. Clutching the shiny bars of the stall with both hands he peered through.

The cream was a gelding, small-boned but with good lines. Jemal-Edin called to him in the Avar language. The horse turned his attention from the flock of visitors down the aisle, looked at the boy and whinnied. Then he bobbed his head as if in greeting and came over to where the boy stood and nuzzled the outstretched hand.

Jemal-Edin caressed the velvety nose. The gelding pulled his lips back to expose his big teeth and then, with a wicked little flick of his head, tried to bite.

The defiant orneriness of the gesture delighted the boy, and he broke into a little cackle of laughter. "This one!" he called to Mahmet. "Tell the White Sultan's son that I choose this one!"

WHEN THEY ARRIVED BACK AT THE SHCHUKIN MANSION
that evening, Jemal-Edin was so tired that he stumbled getting down from the carriage. It embarrassed
him to stumble before the czar's son and Feo. He
picked himself up off the sidewalk before anyone
could help him and hurried up the steps to the house.

He didn't know what was wrong, but his feet were
not doing what he wished them to. When he moved
his head, everything blurred before his eyes. He managed to return the czaravitch's parting bow and stand
at attention as the royal carriage departed. By sheer
willpower he made it into the house, past the door-
man, the footmen, and halfway up the first flight of
stairs. Beside him, but seemingly from a far distance,
Feo was talking. Mahmet was coming up the steps
behind them, dutifully translating. Then Jemal-Edin
quit hearing any voices. The steps in front of him

buckled and dimmed. A veil of black slipped over his eyes and he felt himself falling.

He woke again to hear voices somewhere nearby.

"The boy has lacked proper nourishment for a long time. His constitution has been further weakened by the exposure of his recent journey. His symptoms are those of exhaustion. It is my professional opinion that he should be confined to a sickbed and kept there until further notice. He is to have no excitement. None!"

"But His Majesty wishes him to be in his retinue on Monday night!"

"Impossible. Not unless he also wishes to kill the boy. I will send word to the Winter Palace of my findings."

Jemal-Edin opened his eyes to find that it was dark outside. He was in a big bed in a strange room. By the light of the lamp he could see Nanny, Feo's mother and father, and a strange man standing about his bed.

"He's awake!" There was a world of relief in Nanny's voice. She smiled down at him and gave his shoulder a comforting pat. "You were taken ill," she said, then shook her head apologetically. "Perhaps Mahmet could be allowed in to explain things to him so that he is not frightened?"

Colonel Shchukin nodded approval, and Mahmet was summoned.

"You wore yourself out, boy," Mahmet told him. "Now you must stay in bed until you get some flesh back on your bones."

"But I am well!" Jemal-Edin tried to sit up and the

room blurred again. He fell back onto the big pillow. "I do not want to stay here," he protested.

"But you will," said Mahmet. "The doctor has ordered it. And the more you rest and eat, the better you will be and the sooner you will be up and about again."

"Why can't I rest in the other room—with Feo and Sophia?"

Mahmet relayed the question to the nurse and reported her reply. "They say you can return to the other children in a few days—when you are better. But it is thought Feo and Sophia will be too active and keep you from sleeping as you should. Be patient. It will not be long."

If Mahmet said more than that, Jemal-Edin did not hear it. He had fallen asleep. He slept almost constantly for three days, waking only to go to the bathroom, eat the custards Nanny fed him, submit to a sponge bath and a fresh nightshirt before falling to sleep again. Sometimes he wakened to find Nanny gone from the chair beside the bed. Then one of the maids or Mahmet or even Feo's mama would be sitting with him.

But a morning came when he wakened shortly after dawn to find the chair empty. He looked about the room, found he was alone, and gave an unconscious sigh of relief. Quietly he sat up and listened. The big house was quiet. Cautiously he slid out of bed and stood. The room remained steady. His ears did not buzz. As if experimenting with his strength, he walked over to the window and pushed aside the white curtains to look out onto the courtyard.

The fountain was flashing in the sunlight. Six sea-gulls were standing atop the manure pile in the sta-bleyard, warming their feet. A maid came out of the building across the way, carrying a basket of wet wash which she proceeded to hang on the clothesline by the garden wall. A groom crossed over from the stable to talk with her.

"You should be in your bed, boy," Mahmet's voice came from the bedroom doorway. "You catch cold, too, and your Nanny will blame me. No arguments now. Back under the covers!"

Jemal-Edin went. Not willingly but because Mahmet was too big to argue with. But he resented it. At least something was going on outside there. And when Nanny came in with breakfast of hot custard, he resented that, too. He was feeling better.

Because he was improving, the boredom of being an invalid began to tell on him and he started to brood. He decided he was being treated like a baby. He was fed custards and soups and endless eggs. He was not allowed to get up at dawn, even when they moved him back into the nursery. While Feo and Sophia had their morning lessons, he had to stay in bed and rest. He was ordered to take afternoon naps, and Mahmet, a mere servant, yelled at him when he tried to sneak out of bed. What was more humiliating to him was the fact that he slept in the afternoon, often longer than little Sophia.

He had never before been treated like a real child. At home not only the boys showed deference to him because of his birthright and his well-developed warrior's skills, but their fathers did also. The men knew it would be only a matter of a few years before he rode with them as a man, his father's chief cohort and heir to his father's power. They did nothing to slight the dignity of such potential power and danger to themselves.

And when he was taken hostage and brought north, it was as Shamil's son, not as a child. To Jemal-Edin's way of thinking, the captains had treated him as a man among men. Language and cultural barriers and military protocol helped him to maintain his belief in his own importance. But in this house they apparently cared nothing about Shamil and warrior codes and protocol. Here he was considered sick, which to him was to be thought weak, and he was bundled up in bed and pampered.

"Has my horse arrived from the White Sultan's stables?" he asked Mahmet one morning.

"Not yet," said Mahmet. "You are not allowed out yet anyway."

"When will he be here?"

"How should I know?" Mahmet replied impatiently. He was getting tired of this boring duty and longed to be back at the Winter Palace where something was always happening.

Because Czar Nicholas had given express orders that his new ward's horse was to be delivered complete with appropriate saddles and trappings, custom-made for the boy, there was a bureaucratic delay while every last detail was attended to. No craftsman would risk displeasing the czar. The horse remained at the royal stables awaiting his outfitting. But no one thought to explain this to Jemal-Edin. When several more days had passed and the horse still had not come, Jemal-Edin decided that maybe the whole thing had been an elaborate Infidel gesture to let him know the lack of esteem in which his father and consequently he himself was held.

When he was allowed out of bed, he would curl up and brood on the thickly padded bench of the window seat. There he would stare out across the rooftops. It seemed to him endless rooftops stretched over this flat land. They marked endless buildings on endless streets and uncountable hordes of people. All strange, all penning him in, trapping him here.

With so many empty hours to pass, he became homesick. Now that he had lost them, for the first time he realized the true beauty of his mountains. There the view from his house had never been less than five miles, and usually it was much farther than that. And the horizons, instead of being dull and flat as they were here, were panoramas of snowy peaks stretching into the blue distance. There the air was thin and crisp. Here it was thick and humid from the sea.

The very drinking water offended him. The springs in the mountain villages were fed by snow water distilled through rock. The water was always clear and pure and icy. But St. Petersburg was built on salt marsh, and its water tasted warm and brackish and smelled of ancient bogs. He would drink it only when boiled as tea.

Jemal-Edin had been always taught that the Infidels smelled bad, and he decided that teaching had been right. They smelled of liquor and tobacco and musky perfumes, and their skins were permeated with the richness of the heavy food they ate in quantities that shocked his more Spartan tastes. Both by genetic type and diet, mountain people were lean. Before coming here, he had seen only three fat people in his whole lifetime. He had found them comical and revolting. But here, to his now prejudiced eyes, there were more fat people than thin, and he disapproved of their plumpness as much as his father would have.

He did not brood any more about his family. He guessed they were still alive by virtue of the fact that he was still held hostage. And if they were alive, they must have escaped from Akhulgo. Shamil would take care of them. He sat by his window and brooded about the water, and his horse that was not delivered, and fat people, and his horse, and being treated like a baby, and his horse.

Feo and Sophia, seeing him sit so long alone, would come to him and try to get him to play with them, but he seldom wanted to. He couldn't tell them he didn't understand their games, or see any sense in most of them. Mahmet spent most of his time now in the servant's dining room joking with the maids. That left no way for the children to communicate. After a few days the two Russian children tired of trying to cajol their moody new brother and returned to their usual routines. He was no fun. Even the puppy grew bored with Jemal-Edin's moping and yipped to return to her family.

By the time he had made himself thoroughly unhappy, he began to think about escaping. Shamil had told him to endure captivity with courage and patience, true. He remembered that. And not to use his knife on the Infidels. He had not done that. But while there was no honor in hostages escaping, there was no dishonor if one could do it successfully.

It would be easy enough to get out of this house. But to get out of the city, could he do that? The more he thought about it, the more he thought he could. He recalled that when he was brought here, they had traveled always to the north until reaching Moscow. Then they had driven northwest. All he had to do was reverse that route. There were barricades at the city gates, but he was sure he could pass those. Then he would steal a horse and ride like the wind and they would never find him.

THAT NIGHT HE FOUND HIS CLOTHES BY THE DIM LIGHT
of the icon's glow. He even managed to slip into Nanny's room, scale the armoire and get his dagger.
Wearing one of Feo's heaviest coats as protection
against the cold of nights to come, he tiptoed down
the great stairs to the front door. The footmen were
asleep on the floor, one at the bottom of the steps, the
other in front of the door with a rug wrapped around
him. Jemal-Edin stepped noiselessly over them.

The big double front door was locked and barred.
He managed to slide back the bolt but the lock defeated him. There were few locks at home and he
could not understand why the door would not open
for him. The sleeping footman was too close to risk
any noise by trying to force the door. He gave up and
made his way down the back stairs to the ground
floor.

He had never been down here. The place seemed a

maze of rooms dimly lit by flickering oil lamps in the passageways. After blundering into a room piled to the ceiling with cords of birch, he entered a huge room of shelves. They were stacked with plates, row upon row of plates. Then came serving platters, piled equally high, cups and saucers, glassware and crystal, great platters and sauce bowls, silver tureens and pitchers. For minutes he forgot why he was there, so fascinated was he by this display of wealth. There was enough equipment here to feed his father's army at one sitting, he figured. Or, if sold, to finance at least two major battles. Now he thought he understood why all the doors were so tightly secured. His estimation of Feo's father went up three notches.

Back in the hallway again he opened another door and found himself in a cavernous room. But before he could look around he heard a snore. A woman slept on a pallet near the wall and a man stretched out on a bench beside the door. He crossed the room quietly and tried this door. It opened, but as it did, it brushed against a small bell hung overhead. He was outside! But the tinkle of that bell sounded in his ears like a gong, and his heart bumped in fear. He ran across the courtyard toward the black bars of the front gate.

The gate was shut and chained. The iron bars were wet with fog and cold, and his hands slipped as he tried to climb up.

"Don't do that, boy!" A man stepped out of the shadows near the gate and reached up to grab him. "You might fall and hurt yourself. Come on down!"

Jemal-Edin didn't understand him. He just knew he was about to be stopped. He clung halfway up the gate with his knees gripping a bar. Holding on with one hand, with the other he drew his knife. The man below stepped back.

"Come now—I have no wish to hurt you," he said. He reached into the doorway behind him and brought out a lantern. By its light Jemal-Edin saw the man wore the yellow livery of the household staff, and in his hand he carried a stout wooden club. "You don't know what I'm saying to you, do you?" said the gateman. "Look up there." He held the lantern so that its light gleamed off the sharp lancelike tips of the gate's bars. "You manage to get up there and you risk slipping and impaling yourself on those."

Jemal-Edin could see the danger for himself. He also saw there was no other way out of this end of the courtyard. And with this man standing here, he knew he would never be able to make it to the other end of the yard to see if the gate there was any more promising. At least not this time. Without taking his eyes off his enemy, he sighed and put the dagger back into his belt, let go, and landed lightly on the cobblestones below.

"Good boy," the watchman nodded in approval. "You go back to bed now," he suggested and motioned towards the servants' entrance.

Hesitantly Jemal-Edin started walking in that direction. The man followed behind him. When they were near the door, the man called out a name. After a moment the kitchen door opened and the sleepy servant inside stuck his head out.

"See that he gets back to the nursery in one piece," said the gateman. "He was trying to take a walk. And when you come downstairs again, wake up those lazy night footmen!"

Jemal-Edin passed the servant with head held high. He found his own way back through the first floor to the front stairs, up and up the next flights, back to his room. He was aware that the servant followed him all the way and waited in the top-floor hall until the nursery door shut behind him. He threw himself on his bed with a sigh of disgust and lay there, indignant. While plotting his next escape attempt, he fell back to sleep.

It was late morning when he woke again. He lay for a time listening to the faint sounds of the house. Feo was in the schoolroom with the tutor; Sophia's voice could be heard reciting her French lesson in the room beyond Nanny's. From somewhere on the floor came the rumble and thump of logs for the stoves being piled into a central storage room. Idly he wondered where Nanny was. Nanny! If she saw him dressed like this . . . he felt around beneath the comforter for his dagger. It was gone! He threw off the covers and sat up in panic.

"I put the knife back where it belongs." Mahmet said from the doorway behind him. "I also covered you so that no one could see how you were dressed. Get in there and change before anyone else sees you!"

"You are only a servant. You cannot order me about." Jemal-Edin was indignant in his guilt.

"If you are as smart as I think you are, you will not argue with me," replied Mahmet, in no mood to be intimidated. "You will do as I say! Now move! Or big as you are, I will paddle your rear as it should be paddled!"

Jemal-Edin looked at the man. There was a definite grimness about Mahmet's mouth that convinced the boy to obey.

"The night watchman has not told anyone of your attempt to escape. Except myself. And I will tell no one unless I think it necessary," Mahmet said as Jemal-Edin undressed. "What you tried to do was very foolish. Had you succeeded in running away it might have meant your death and the ruin of this house! Did you stop to think about that?"

"I do not believe you," said Jemal-Edin. "I only wanted to go home. And I could do it, too. And I will!"

"And how would Shamil Imam treat a noble who let one of his important hostages escape?"

"Why he would behead him as a traitor . . ." Jemal-Edin's voice trailed into thoughtful silence.

"Do you think Czar Nicholas would be more lenient than Shamil? I can tell you that he is not! Had you gained your freedom, you would have brought disaster on this illustrious family. A family that has shown you nothing but kindness. Is this how you repay kindness?"

Jemal-Edin stared up at the man, his eyes wide with guilt and partial disbelief. When he met him, the White Sultan had seemed like a more forgiving man than Shamil . . . but then, he thought, Shamil could also be as kind as he was cruel. And the White Sultan was much more powerful than Shamil . . .

"Even if the story never went any further than this household, what do you think would happen to the servants—to Nanny especially—since they are responsible too for you? Or don't you care about them either?"

"I never thought . . ."

"No? His Majesty asked you to conduct yourself with honor. Your own father would expect no less. Yet you sit up here and you sulk like a spoiled child— watch out! You are putting the wrong leg into your trousers. You sit here sulking and acting suspicious of every word said to you. Why? These people have nothing to gain by taking advantage of you. They are merely trying to make you feel at home."

"But this is not my home! I do not like it here! I want to go back!"

"But you cannot! Understand that! Not for so long as your father refuses to surrender! You say you want to go home, but when your past returns to you in dreams, you cry out in fear. Do you know that? I know; I have sat beside you and heard your cries. You must remember the past as it was! Not as you wish it to be when you are awake."

Mahmet watched as Jemal-Edin poured water from the fat porcelain pitcher and washed his hands and face in the bowl. The boy was trying hard to show he did not care what Mahmet said. This irritated the man. "Suppose, my Avar friend," he taunted him, "you had succeeded in getting over the gate? How far do you think you would have gotten? You cannot speak Russian. You could not even ask simple directions when you became lost. And you surely would have become lost."

"I would not!"

Mahmet gave a snort of derisive laughter. "Oh, I know you could find your way through any wild country. But you know nothing about cities. Do you know what happens to a boy wandering alone and lost here? In a day you would be caught and tied to some peasant's hut and used as a kitchen serf or a stable boy. Or worse! They would beat you like a dog when you disobeyed!"

"I would kill them! I am the son of Shamil!"

Mahmet laughed again. "And how would you tell them that? By sign language? Who understands you, other than myself?" At that, Jemal-Edin's glance met his for a moment. Mahmet saw a look of despair in the boy's eyes as he realized the truth of what he was being told. Mahmet's tone softened. He was not deliberately trying to be cruel. He too had come to St. Petersburg an exile.

"Why have you not learned any Russian? It has been a month now and more. Do you think by refusing to do so, you will somehow go home sooner? You will not. If you keep this up, when you are sent back, it will be as if you had traveled like a man blind and deaf. Your ignorance of Russian ways will not help your father or his cause. Destiny has brought you here. Into exile, yes. But she could have as easily brought you into slavery or death. Instead His Majesty received you with honor—"

There were footsteps in the nursery, and Nanny

appeared in the dressing room doorway. "I thought I heard you talking with our boy," she said to Mahmet. "Is he ill or just a sleepyhead this morning?"

"He is very well. Just lazy," said Mahmet. "It is my opinion he has recovered. Time begins to weigh heavily on his hands, so he sleeps or broods it away. Perhaps the mistress would allow him to begin some schooling soon?"

For the first time Jemal-Edin found himself making an effort to understand what the two adults were saying. The truth in Mahmet's words was beginning to seep through his resentment.

For the next two days he was his usual preoccupied self, sitting alone on his window seat. But it was with a difference now. "Remember the past as it was, not as you wish it to be," Mahmet had said. Jemal-Edin was trying to do that. To his surprise he found that thinking of much of the past made him very sad. And it was as frightening to remember awake as it was in his dreams. He remembered his fear of the Infidels, his panic when Shamil told him he was to go to them. He had always hated Infidels. Every Murid did. Infidels were all that was evil. And Russians were Infidels —most of them, anyway.

But Nanny was an Infidel and she was as good to him as his own mother. Feo and Sophia were Infidels. "The swish of the sword of Lord Allah on the necks of unbelievers is pious and righteous!" So Shamil had always said. So Jemal-Edin had unquestioningly believed. Feo and Sophia were unbelievers . . . Jemal-Edin knew he could not bear to see them killed. Or their parents. Even Mahmet. Did people remain enemies only so long as you did not know them?

On the third morning after his escape attempt Jemal-Edin called for Mahmet. "I wish you to teach me Russian," he said. "There is much I have to learn!"

THE RIVER NEVA WAS CHOPPY AND SILVER IN THE AFTER-
noon light. Gray clouds of autumn fog were swiftly
moving in from the Gulf of Finland. But in the enormous square before the Winter Palace the weather
was ignored. There, for as far as the eye could see,
rank upon rank of uniformed horsemen paraded in
extravagant difficult drills. Ten cavalry regiments rode
in formation, diverged, wheeled in intricate patterns,
and merged again into rank. No officer's voice could
be heard. The clang of horseshoes on cobblestones
echoed and re-echoed back from the façades of the
palaces hemming the square.

Out for the first time since his recovery, Jemal-Edin
sat with Mahmet, Feo, and Feo's mother in an open
carriage. They were parked to the right of the reviewing stand. Their carriage was surrounded by those of
other nobles whose wives and children had come
down to watch the review.

As Jemal-Edin watched he was awed, as all were meant to be, by the sight of so large a mounted army drilling with such clockwork precision. He could feel the pavement below vibrating with the weight of the horsemen.

A fanfare of trumpets rang out over the clatter. The horsemen wheeled and cantered to the far end of the square and, at a second blare, wheeled again and trotted forward toward the reviewing stand. Up there, plainly visible in a red uniform, stood the Commander in Chief of all the Armies of Russia, Czar Nicholas I, playing soldiers with the ultimate equipment.

The trumpets sang out again. With well-practiced ease officers rode two lengths forward while their men reined left and passed in orderly formation down the Nevsky Prospect. Smartly side-stepping their horses, the officers formed rank and then, upon the trumpet call, spurred their mounts and galloped at top speed, still in precision rank, as if to an attack.

When it looked to the inexperienced Jemal-Edin as if the horses would pound right over them all and crash against the stone barrier of the palace walls themselves, the czar calmly raised his saber. The officers pulled their horses up short. The animals reared and pawed the air, whickering in alarm and pain as tight bits cut into their tongues, their horseshoes making one final *clonk* on the stone pavement. The officers had halted with all lines within each rank a fraction of an inch of being even. All except for one unfortunate colonel.

He was in the front row, exposed to the full view of

the czar. The colonel's horse had slipped as it reared, tottered on one hind leg for a sickening instant, and then fell backwards onto the pavement. The rider was barely able to jump clear of his mount before it rolled and scrambled back up onto its feet and stood shaking in fright.

In a minute where all had been noise and movement, all was silence in the great square. The czar ignored the faultless performance of the rest of his ranked thousands that day. He strode over to the edge of the platform nearest the colonel who had marred the event.

"You there!" he shouted. "Advance!" His voice echoed in the stillness. The man came forward leading his limping stallion. When he stood directly beneath his emperor, he saluted and then awaited the imperial wrath.

"Have you no other mounts?" inquired the czar.

"I have five others, Your Imperial Highness."

"Yet you chose to ride this one today?"

"Yes, Your Imperial Highness."

"Before *me*?"

"I most sincerely regret my poor performance, Your Imperial Highness, and humbly beg your forgiveness."

The czar glared down at him for a long moment. "You will return to your barracks," he said finally. "We do not wish to see you again until you have learned how to ride."

Dismissed, the miserable officer saluted again, turned, and led his now unridable stallion away, across the vast square past his fellow officers until the lonely sound of his footsteps and the faltering clip-clop-clop of his horse's hoofs died away in the distance.

As he watched the disgraced man go, Jemal-Edin felt sorry for him. He was wondering if he could have stopped even Baba on so short a notice and decided he probably could not have done so. He did not think the emperor unfair in humiliating the man. One did not pass judgment on such power. Instead he resolved that he himself would become so good a horseman that never would he be humiliated like this.

The military review continued, infantry following cavalry, artillery regiments following dragoons, until even the boys lost interest. While Feo talked to a friend in the next carriage, Jemal-Edin turned his attention to the people in the reviewing stand. Behind the emperor's retinue sat a number of ladies and gentlemen of the court, nobles of various rank, visiting foreign dignitaries, chamberlains, and ambassadors. Few of them were watching the troops parade either. Some were chatting among themselves, others with opera glasses were scanning the carriages drawn up below and waving to acquaintances they spotted. Some of them were looking at the Shchukin carriage. One old woman in particular seemed to have her opera glasses trained on him.

As she saw him looking, she put down the glasses and stared directly at him with no pretense of subtlety. Then she got up and gathered her skirts about her in preparation to leave. "Is she coming down here?" he wondered. As she rose, two young women sitting beside her also rose. There was some conversation. One young woman took the old lady's arm. She pulled roughly away and gave the young woman a shove.

An officer caught the girl as she fell, steadied her, and then turned his attention to the old woman. Another man hurried up, and the two of them, with some difficulty, escorted the old woman off the reviewing stand and into the doorway of the palace behind them.

Jemal-Edin found their treatment of her very curious. There was something vaguely familiar about her. She reminded him in a way of his grandmother, Shamil's mother, who was also a fiery old lady. He wondered if she, too, was from his mountains and if so, had they ever met. She seemed to know him. He glanced over at Mahmet and saw that he too was watching the scene.

"Who is she?" he asked.

"A . . . a noblewoman from Georgia," Mahmet said guardedly. "A most extraordinary woman."

"What is her name?"

Mahmet shrugged. "I cannot tell you that. I do not know if His Majesty wishes you to know of her."

Jemal-Edin had to accept that. But at least learning she was from Georgia explained her familiar air. Georgia was the small and ancient kingdom bordering Daghestan, next to the Black Sea. From early on Jemal-Edin had heard tales of its wealth, of its rich farms and orchards, its fat cattle and sheep and goats. Some of Shamil's most profitable raids took place in Georgia.

"Is she visiting the court?" he persisted.

Mahmet permitted himself a half-smile. "Yes," he said. "You could say she is here on an extended visit. Look!" He pointed out toward the parade ground, "Those are the Don Cossack regiments, the finest fighting men in all Russia!"

Jemal-Edin had the feeling Mahmet had deliberately changed the subject but he didn't know why. They would soon meet, the old woman and the boy, but it would be years before he heard her story.

For the old woman was Marie, the last queen of Georgia. When her husband died, she had learned to her great rage that neither she nor her sons would inherit the throne. To avoid an otherwise inevitable Russian invasion, King George had signed a treaty with the czar making Georgia a Russian protectorate.

Queen Marie had refused to accept that situation. She and her sons plotted against the Russian viceroy. At last the Russians lost patience. The royal family was asked to vacate their palace and retire to a country estate east of Tiflis. This too Marie refused to do. She took to her bed and refused to grant an audience to Russian emissaries.

Weeks passed and finally Russian troops surrounded her palace and entered its halls. Two very noble Russian officers sent a chamberlain in to tell her that, although they regretted doing so, they were ordered to advise her that if she did not get up, get dressed, and get out, they would be forced to lift her bodily from her royal bed and place her in her royal coach.

"Let them try!" said Queen Marie and she stayed put.

The two officers duly entered her bed chamber and pleaded with her to leave in dignity. She spat at them in reply. The man in charge leaned over the bed and attempted to lift her. From beneath her pillows she whipped out a Turkish scimitar and disembowled the unfortunate fellow, then stabbed his cohort through the chest. Her sons, hidden behind the curtains about her bed, sprang out with daggers drawn and slaughtered five other Russian officers who came running in at hearing the death cries. In the melée that followed, several of her young sons were killed and Queen Marie was taken prisoner.

Royalty would not willingly kill royalty. The czar ordered the queen to be shackled and marched in chains across Russia. If she died on the trip, her death would be an act of God. But the queen made the trip, in winter, and survived to spit on the floor at the czar's feet. She was sent to a convent and kept there in seclusion for more than twenty years. Only when Nicholas I came to the throne was she released and allowed an apartment at court. Even there she was watched constantly, for Marie was still a queen terrible in her thirst for vengeance for her lost kingdom.

Wild shouts rang out from the square now as the Cossacks were replaced by a horde of young warriors from the Transcaucasus and the lands to the north and east. For these troops Jemal-Edin noted, there was no Prussian discipline. They rode here as they did at home, in a wild breakneck rush, brandishing their sabers and shrieking battle cries.

To pay their respects to the czar, they galloped past him in a mass, shrilling ululations so fierce that some

of the watching ladies looked about to reassure themselves that civilized and well-armed Russian officers
stood near at hand to defend them should these wild-
men run amok.

Jemal-Edin stared at them too, but in surprise instead of fear. For among these troops were many
Tchetchins whom he had believed loyal to Shamil.
His heart sank a little. He had not known so many
tribesman had gone over to the Russian side. Many of
the riders wore costumes strange to him; there were
so many different tribes. And from their hair and
dress, it was apparent these young men were only the
nobles' sons. His opinion of the White Sultan rose.
The man must surely be powerful to command the
loyalty of so many rich men.

Beside him Feo was watching the Tatar and Mon-
gol troops in fascination. "I should like to ride like
they do," he told Jemal-Edin in admiration. "You are
very lucky! They are the only group that looks as if
they are having fun!" He said something more, and
his mother interrupted him.

"What did they say?" Jemal-Edin asked Mahmet.

Mahmet reported the first part of Feo's speech.
"But I cannot tell you the rest because it will spoil a
surprise," he said.

"What surprise?" asked Jemal-Edin, but his words
were drowned out by the shrill of the horsemen as
they massed into a semblance of order before the reviewing stand. The czar regarded them tolerantly; he
was too shrewd to try to impose on these men of a
different culture a Western idea of warfare. They had
won too many battles for him to interfere with the

command of their generals as he commonly did with his other armies.

Now Nicholas stalked over to the balustrade nearest the carriage in which Jemal-Edin sat. Peering down, the czar called out a command. A small detachment of palace guards approached the carriage. The footman opened the door. Madame Shchukin rose and stepped out, then held out her hands for her son and Jemal-Edin.

Flanked by the guards, she led the boys up the steps to the reviewing stand. There the czar bowed to her with great civility and saluted both boys. Then, to Jemal-Edin's confusion, the man took his arm and led only him over to center stage. Mahmet followed at a respectful distance. Nicholas barked out another order. The assembled troops saluted and fell back. An avenue opened in their ranks which stretched across to the entrance of the riding academy in the old Michael Palace.

There, being led across the square, was a cream-colored horse. As it grew closer Jemal-Edin saw that it was his gelding. The White Sultan had kept his promise! The horse's coat had been brushed until it gleamed, its mane and tail bleached and braided with red ribbons. It was outfitted with a red leather saddle trimmed with brushed gold and bridle and stirrups to match.

"Ahhhh!" Jemal-Edin gave a long sigh of pleasure.

Nicholas looked down at him and smiled for the first time that afternoon. "Does it please you?" he asked. Jemal-Edin was so entranced by the beauty of the animal that he did not hear the question the first time, and the czar had to repeat it.

"It is the gift one would give a prince!" he said fervently.

"And so you are," said Nicholas. "To show my esteem for you and your people, while you are my guest in Russia you will bear the title of Coronet Prince—a prince of the crown. To you will be granted the privileges and responsibilities of that title."

As Mahmet translated this speech he added his own instructions to Jemal-Edin. "Now you kneel and thank him for this great honor. Believe me, it is one conferred upon few!"

Jemal-Edin knelt before the czar. "You are most generous, Great White Sultan," he said. "As you honor me in your kindness, so you honor my noble father, the Imam Shamil, and my noble mother, Fatimat. Could they know of your kindness to me, they would be most impressed, as I am. And most grateful, as I am. When I return to my homeland, I will tell them your power is exceeded only by your generosity . . ."

Here Mahmet interrupted and began translating the boy's reply to Nicholas. He knew an Avar could make a thank-you speech more elaborate than any gift. When he had finished the czar smiled and did something quite remarkable for so customarily stiff a man as he. He lifted Jemal-Edin to his feet and kissed him on both cheeks. Then, putting his arm around Jemal-Edin's shoulders, said, "We shall go down and see if the stirrups are the right length for you."

Together, man and boy walked down the steps. Like a proud father, Nicholas watched as Jemal-Edin swung up easily into the saddle, took hold of the crimson silk reins and patted the nervous horse reassuringly on the neck.

Years later Jemal-Edin would look back on this bittersweet moment and wonder what the rest of the watching court had thought of this gesture of the czar's—and what impression it had made on the Tatar troops. How long had it taken for the report of this scene to reach the ears of Shamil? And, as it did, how many of the watching warriors were really Shamil's spies?

But at that moment he only wished he was alone on the square so that he might test the speed of this beautiful horse. As if reading his thoughts, Nicholas said, "The animal might shy at this crowd, my son. You dismount now. One of the palace grooms will follow your carriage home and lead your horse." He watched Jemal-Edin dismount, then walked with him and the Shchukins to the yellow carriage.

On the way home Jemal-Edin and Feo knelt on the carriage seat, looking back at the horse being led behind them and the cart which followed, loaded with new tack. Jemal-Edin smiled all the way home.

THE FRONT ENTRANCE OF THE SHCHUKIN TOWNHOUSE was flanked by twin balustraded steps, curving from the first floor to the street. Carriages stopped here for the gentry to alight. Serfs, servants, and delivery van drivers rang the bell for the watchman to admit them through high iron gates into the courtyard. Behind the house stretched a large walled formal garden with a back gate opening into the kitchen garden nestled for warmth against the stable walls. House, gardens, stables, greenhouse, carriage house, and the long three-story building for the many servants formed a comfortable square complex around an inner court-yard paved in brick. In the center of the courtyard a small flower garden encircled a fountain from Italy.

The rear gate from the courtyard led into a tree-shaded park. It was here Jemal-Edin rode each morning, sometimes with Feo. More often alone.

He was awake before dawn. Only the burning candle in its red glass before the icon lit the room. He listened and the house was quite still. Beside him Saidia stirred and tried to worm closer. He sat up, encircled the puppy with his arm, and slid her off the pillow and under the covers. She snuffled and went into a deeper sleep. He swung his legs over the edge of the bed, being careful not to make the covers rustle.

Feo slept soundly in the bed next to his, mouth slightly open, breathing deep and even. Jemal-Edin tiptoed across the room and listened at Nanny's door for the comforting sound of her soft snore. As he turned to cross to the dressing room and get his clothes, he saw that Sophia in her alcove bed had, as usual, kicked off her covers. She was just like his little brother, he thought and smiled to himself. She slept huddled in a ball, her voluminous nightdress wrapped tightly around her toes, scant protection against the morning breeze beginning to come in the window. He went over and slowly pulled her comforter up and tucked it about her small shoulders. He had no more than finished when she turned over with a flop that made him jump back.

"Please, Allah," he prayed in silence, "do not let her waken. She will want to go along with me." His prayer was answered. Like the puppy, as soon as the little girl felt the warmth of the covers, she snuggled into them and slept on.

Behind the closed door of the dressing room he removed his long nightshirt, poured water from the pitcher into the silver basin and washed the sleep from his face before going into the toilet chamber. He considered it a great luxury, this toilet chamber. It had a tapestry-covered seat with a lid concealing a round hole cut into the center and a chamber pot positioned beneath, and hidden behind, a cupboard door. In his homeland such things were unheard of. There he had either used the pit in the corner of the sleeping room, which had a drain to the gutter in the street outside, or if the need were more serious, went outside to the rough unroofed shelter perched on the very edge of the cliff. With the snows of winter this privy was not only very cold, but quite dangerous, since a child could lose his grip and slip through the hole and fall down into the river chasm below. When he was little, he remembered having nightmares about falling from that drafty perch. Even now he thought of it with a shudder.

He dressed and carried his boots from the room, through the nursery and out into the hall. Down the stairs and along the gallery, to the left, into the warming pantry, and down another stairs to the kitchen in the ground floor. There he sat down on a bench and pulled on his boots.

The kitchen was his favorite room in the house. It was huge and well lit by windows and contained three modern wood-burning ranges of cast iron trimmed with brass. Feo said they had come all the way from England. Down the center of the room ran a long, wide worktable. Above it, from a pipe bent into a rectangle and suspended on chains from the high ceiling, hung a great variety of pots, pans, graters, shredders, and strainers. On the walls in neat racks, arranged both for use and size, were the kitchen knives and choppers. Next to the deep sinks stood a wooden pump, the first Jemal-Edin had ever seen, to draw water from the cistern. On a table by itself gleamed the bulging brass samovar, the glowing coals in its belly still hot enough to make it steam.

He went over to it now, spooned some tea into a small pot and filled the pot with hot water. Setting the tea on the worktable to steep, he opened a cupboard and found the bread and honey. As the cupboard door latch clicked shut, the night cook sleeping on a palleted bench next to one of the ranges stirred and turned over. She opened one eye, saw who it was, gave a blurry smile that showed two front teeth missing and went back to sleep.

Jemal-Edin was on good terms with the house staff, even the butler and the French chef. He was quiet and polite, not like the sons of some of the aristocrats they served. They were not sure where he came from, or what he was doing in the Shchukin household, but they liked him. And he liked them. They were not like the slaves his father kept as servants. His father's slaves lived very miserable lives and, as a result, were very unpleasant people. And while the boy was not sure if these servants were slaves or not, in this rich household he thought they were far better off than any mountain noble he had ever seen.

The sky was barely light when he finished his hurried meal and went out by the kitchen door into the courtyard. Sparrows were waking in the eaves of the stable. An autumn fog from the Baltic lay lightly over the city. He paused for a moment to look out the big gate at a train of ox carts passing the house, their high wooden wheels creaking under towering loads of wood from the forests east of the city. Winter was coming with its snow and bitter cold. St. Petersburg warmed itself on wood. The oxen and the serfs who drove them made endless trips to supply that wood.

A driver in a massive sheepskin coat, his feet wrapped in rags, saw the boy standing there behind the great gate and waved a silent greeting. Jemal-Edin waved back. As he did so he felt for the first time since he had left home a sense of belonging, belonging to this house, to these strange, but kind, people. And for the first time in his life, he was aware of being happy.

In the stables one of the old grooms was awake and working. His name was Ivan and he was one of Jemal-Edin's special friends along with Feo, Sophia, and Nanny. The old man had spent his life with horses. His knowledge of them and love for them was great. Born a serf on the Shchukin estate at Kaluga, he had been brought by Feo's grandfather to the house in St. Petersburg. He told Jemal-Edin that he liked being a city man and said the boy would also, as soon as he became used to the noise. But like the boy, he still missed the country at dawn.

The two of them chattered to each other eagerly, only hindered at times by Jemal-Edin's still sketchy command of Russian. Ivan put down his wooden fork, and together they saddled Djinn. Ivan led the animal out into the courtyard for the boy to mount, then went over and opened the gate to the park.

"You be careful now," Ivan told him. "None of that trick riding I saw you doing the other morning. Going as fast as you can standing up in the stirrups and then sliding under his belly! If you break your fool neck I will be flogged for helping you do it. I have never been flogged and I'm too old to learn to take to it."

"But I am only just beginning to train him," objected Jemal-Edin. "What you have seen me do is nothing. It takes very long to train a horse to stop quickly without throwing his rider, to rear and turn without falling on his side, and not to lessen his pace when the rider jumps off and jumps back on again."

"You are going to teach Djinn to do all that?" Ivan asked skeptically.

"And more!" the boy assured him. "You should see some of the fighting stallions of the khans! When they go into battle they are greater warriors than their riders. They rear and scream and kick out at their enemy, trying to break the other horses' legs. When an enemy rider falls, they wheel and trample him. They bite and use their heads as well as their hoofs as weapons. They are truly wonderful horses!" he said, his eyes bright as he remembered them.

Ivan shook his head in disapproval. "Is that what you want this horse to be? A warrior?"

"Oh no," Jemal-Edin assured him. "When a stallion is trained to such ferocity, you cannot stable him with riding horses. He would kick down his stall and kill them all if he could."

The old groom looked up at the bright-eyed boy and in his face was a look Jemal-Edin often saw in the faces of these adults when he spoke unguardedly of his past life. A mixture of wonder and puzzlement.

Ivan shook his head. "Did they give you no time to be a child?" he asked softly.

"Excuse me, my Russian is poor as yet," Jemal-Edin said, not understanding the old man's meaning.

"Nothing, boy," said Ivan. "You go on with your ride now. And watch yourself. This horse is still too big for you."

They galloped twice around the park, Djinn releasing in joyful running the great energy generated by confinement in his stall for the night. After the second turn about, he slowed to canter along the bridle path among the pines.

Jemal-Edin enjoyed these lonely morning rides. It was the only time of day when he could be by himself. His days now were very busy. Since Mahmet had gone, there was the daily Russian lesson with André, then four hours spent with the tutor and Feo in the schoolroom next to the nursery, boring fitting sessions with tailors, bootmakers, and hatters. These people made life very difficult by having different clothing for everything they did.

Everything was new and very different. A great deal of time was spent merely eating. Here women ate with men, but children ate with their nurses or their tutors. At home his father ate alone, behind a low table, seated on the floor mats. His mother, along with Javaret, ate only when all the men had been fed, but before the slaves, who were given the left-overs.

Then there was the matter of religion. Jemal-Edin had not knelt toward Mecca to pray since beginning the trip north. He had prayed once, on the floor of the carriage. The Russian officers had laughed. He did not make that mistake again. But if they found his religion a source of laughter, he in turn found their habit of praying to wooden pictures and statues just as silly. The people who were the subjects of these panel pictures called icons, although they were crowned with gold, often looked very sick, and some of them seemed to him to look like beggars. The village gatemen would have set the dogs on anyone who arrived looking like that.

He had gone once with Feo, Sophia, and Nanny to the great cathedral that stood by the river. He had marveled at the colors of the stained glass pictures of hollow-eyed Infidel mollahs, admired the weaving skills in the rich tapestries, the beauty of the golden and jeweled vessels and the ornate altars. But the uncluttered simplicity of the great mosque appealed to him far more.

What was most different of all was the living habits of these Russians. He had always been taught that food was a necessity, a thing to be eaten only so that one could remain alive. But the Russians seemed to live for food; the richer, the more elaborate, the better. He was accustomed to meat either roasted or skewered in small pieces and grilled over open flames. Here their meats were chopped and diced and mixed with other ingredients, cooked in oil or smothered in cream sauces and rich gravies so that one could never be sure that he was eating. Twice he had eaten and enjoyed pork without being aware of it until too late.

And the Russians turned night into day. They

would sleep all day, have breakfast at six in the evening, then bathe, dress and rest until going to dine with friends at eleven at night. Their parties never ended until the small hours of the morning. Jemal-Edin thought perhaps it was due to the influence of having chandeliers and oil lamps in their houses. Only the serfs, the servants, and peasants rose early in the morning to handle the work of their world. And Czar Nicholas—who told Jemal-Edin he rose punctually at five each morning and went to work at his desk. This habit, he said, made him quite unpopular with his staff since it kept them from enjoying any social life whatever.

When he thought about it all, Jemal-Edin found it very confusing. So he tried to accept it and become one of them.

The bridle path led to a meadow beside a small lake. Here, after stopping a time to watch the last of the migrating ducks and geese who swam on the lake and searched for food along its edges, he set to work teaching Djinn the things every good Avar horse must know.

JEMAL-EDIN NEVER GOT OVER BEING ASTOUNDED BY THE very size of the Winter Palace. He could see it distorted through the rain-jeweled window of the imperial coach. The palace stood on the Prospect, overlooking the Neva, opposite the Fortress of Peter and Paul. Three stories high, of maroon-painted marble, its quarter-mile length almost dwarfed the other great stone palaces along the Prospect. Along its rooftop the statues mounted there seemed to be moving against the scudding gray clouds, perhaps watching their images reflected in the wet pavement below.

In his white-gloved hand, the boy clutched the written invitation from the wife of the Great White Sultan. He could not as yet read it, but Mama, Feo's mother, had told him that the czarina said she wished to meet this boy of whom her husband spoke so fondly. And she wished to meet him at once. Accordingly, the coach that delivered the invitation waited for him to dress and be driven back to the Winter Palace for this honor.

Or at least Mama seemed to think it was an honor. Jemal-Edin was not sure of that as yet. He had planned to spend this late afternoon after his lessons in the tackroom with Feo, helping the harnessmaker design a special bit for Djinn. Now that would have to wait. Besides, he felt at home in the tackroom. Here in this upholstered coach, seated between two strange men in palace uniform, he felt stiff and ill at ease.

At the palace the coach drew up under a porte-cochere. He and his escorts got out, and he was led inside into the vast echoing marble and mirrored halls, full as always of men in military uniform hurrying along importantly, pages darting by, lackeys in livery with dignified tread, courtiers going nowhere in particular, Cossacks, Tarters, Nubians in enormous turbans, ladies of the court rustling past in silken splendour. Twice his escorts had to stop and wait for him to finish staring with open mouth at someone or something he had seen.

They passed the open doors of a huge room paneled entirely in the rich green of malachite. Jemal-Edin darted inside to look. He took off his right glove and felt the gleaming texture of the stone, then polished his fingermarks away with the glove. The finish was too beautiful to mar. At one end of the room, on a matching pedestal, stood a malachite urn large enough to hold several men. "Who lifted it up there?"

he wanted to know, never doubting that somewhere in this marvelous kingdom there must be a giant capable of that feat.

His little entourage came to a wide marble stairs flanked at intervals by uniformed guards, standing beneath oil lamps that were mounted on the walls. Since the day was gloomy, the lamps were lit, their oil floating in a layer above the water that kept them from overheating and cracking and causing fires.

Down another hall and then to a double door, flanked by guards, to the private apartment of the czarina. He was shown into an anteroom and left standing there to wait alone, except for the ever-present guard who stared straight ahead and pretended he was part of the furniture. In a few moments there was a rustle of silk and a tall, slender, rather plain-looking woman, smelling of perfume and pastry, swept in. She was dressed in lavender; her belt, buttons, brooch, and bracelet were of Siberian amethyst set in heavy silver.

She smiled and greeted him in French. Seeing he did not understand, she repeated in Russian, "I am so very glad you came, Prince Jemal. I have so long wished to meet you."

He swept off his hat and bowed very solemnly, as Feo and André, the tutor, had taught him, but before he could recite the small speech of greeting they had made him rehearse at the last minute, the empress reached out a hand glittering with rings and took his arm. "Shall we go inside to my study?" she said, and before he could reply, led him through the door, across a high-ceilinged, gilt-trimmed room whose parquet floor was covered with a fine Persian carpet, past another pair of house guards, into a small, heavily carpeted, richly draped chamber.

They sat on a delicate gilt settee upholstered in silk. Jemal-Edin had to grasp the arm firmly and push himself back into the far recesses of the seat to keep from sliding off the slippery fabric. The drapes were drawn, shutting out the cold and rain, and the soft glow of lamplight filled the room. Although a tall porcelain stove in one corner of the room provided adequate heat, the empress had a fire burning in the fireplace. On a low table before them was an ornate gold tea service.

"I was just about to have some pastry and tea," the empress said, removing the linen napkin from a tray to expose a succulent-looking strudel. "Like yourself, I was not born in Russia. Sometimes I miss the foods of my childhood. When I am alone, which is rare when we are here at Court, I like to indulge myself. Have you ever tasted apple strudel?" She handed him a slice on a gold plate with a golden fork.

"No, Your Majesty," said Jemal-Edin, shaking his head.

"I think you will like it," she assured him. "It is made of apples—you know what apples are?" He nodded. "And raisins and nuts."

He attempted to cut off a bite with his fork, rather awkwardly since forks were still uncomfortable for him and he was afraid of slipping off the settee besides. The delicate crust of the pastry proved remarkably resistant to his attack. Finally he managed. The look that came over his face as the sugary strudel, still warm from the oven, melted on his tongue brought a smile to the face of his hostess.

"It *is* good, is it not?" she said.

"It is the best thing I have ever eaten!" he said. And it was.

The empress looked sideways at him as she leaned forward to pour the tea, and saw how precariously he was managing to balance the plate to eat and still retain his seat. "I am sorry," she said, "perhaps you would be more comfortable sitting on a cushion on the floor? You can put your plate on the table . . . here, like this, as my children do." She moved his plate for him as he slid off the settee and settled gratefully onto the fat cushion she pointed to. "Yes," she nodded watching him fold his legs beneath him. "That looks far more comfortable. Now tuck your napkin there, over your lap, in case a bit slips off your fork. Strudel is delicious, but it is messy."

"You remind me of my . . ." He paused, remembering that the people here avoided mentioning his family. It was as if he had had no other life before he came here so far as they were concerned. "Of someone I used to know," he concluded rather lamely.

"Do you miss your mother very much?" she asked and she seemed genuinely concerned.

"Sometimes," he admitted, his brown eyes clouding over.

"Yes, I would imagine you do. I used to miss my mother very much when I first came to Russia. And I came by my own choice. Well," she said brightening, "we shall try to make it up to you. My son tells me that you are a very fine rider. He was greatly impressed with your skill that day you met and rode at the stables. What did you name your horse?"

"Djinn—because Ivan says a djinn can be both good and evil. But he is mostly good. You should see him in the morning . . ."

Jemal-Edin forgot his awe of this woman and began to talk to her as freely as he talked with Nanny. And he saw the czarina seemed to listen closely and was interested in what he said, her eyes watching his as he spoke, her head trembling slightly on her long neck. In his innocence, he imagined it was he that made her nervous and he made as great an effort to be as gentle as he would with a frightened animal.

To him the guards that constantly surrounded the imperial family were simply decorative, a mark of power and prestige. It never occured to him they served the same purpose as his father's bodyguards. He knew nothing of the violence of the past that made these guards necessary or of the spirit of revolt that brewed beneath the surface glitter of wealth and power and absolute tyrannical rule.

When Nicholas entered the room almost an hour later, he found the two of them there, both sitting on the floor, the gleaming skirts of the czarina's gown almost covering Jemal-Edin's legs, their heads bent over an elaborate picture book of animals, his wife telling the boy of a pet marmoset she had had as a child.

"I see he has charmed you as well," Nicholas said affably, his tall figure looming over them in startling unexpectedness and then, as his wife stiffled a cry of surprise and sprang up in flustered alarm, he said "I am sorry, my dear. You were so engrossed in your story I hated to interrupt. No . . . no . . . stay where you are, Prince Jemal-Edin," he said as the boy rose to his feet and bowed ceremoniously. "In this room we forget some of the discipline that is necessary in public." And then added sternly, "But only a little of that discipline."

"We are having such a nice visit, Nicholas," said the czarina. "Jemal-Edin is a very bright young man. He has learned Russian so quickly. I find it a pleasure to speak with him."

"Then by all means, we must have him visit us more often," said the czar, settling himself comfortably on a lounge.

"And I think it would be wise for him to begin learning French and German if he is to become a member of the Court. Do you not agree?"

"Certainly! We shall enroll him in the Cadet Corps School very soon as well. Would you like that, my boy?"

"I do not know, sire," said Jemal-Edin. "What is the Cadet School?"

"It is a very great honor!" replied Nicholas. "My finest officers began their careers in my schools—nowhere else! The military is the only career for a real man. To suceed as an officer, to command men, to fight and die for God and your czar, that is the finest of goals!"

"Nicholas," the empress gently pleaded, "Jemal-Edin is only a boy."

But the boy saw nothing wrong in what the czar suggested. What he had said was simply another version of what Shamil always said, that for a warrior to die for Allah and the Imam Shamil was to enter Paradise.

"He is the same age as the Grand Duke Michael, is he not?" asked Nicholas. "Our son is proving to be a fine cadet. So will this boy. As my ward and protégé, Jemal-Edin, there will be no path not open to you, should you wish to take advantage of it. Some day, of course, you will return to Daghestan, and if you prove to be the man I think you capable of being, you will return as the viceroy of the Caucasus or at least governor general of Daghestan. Your return will bring peace and prosperity. My subjects shall bless your name as they bless my own."

"And my father the Imam, what Russian title and honors shall he hold, sire?" asked the puzzled boy.

The czar stood up, abruptly ending his visit. "You must invite our guest to the cottage at Peterhof, my dear," he said to his wife, smiling down at Jemal-Edin in lieu of a reply to the boy's question. Jemal-Edin smiled back rather hesitantly; he had the impression that he had in some way offended the White Sultan. The empress saw her husband to the door of the study, and when she returned Jemal-Edin noted that her face seemed flushed. They talked of military school for a little time, and then she rang for a lady-in-waiting to summon a maid to summon a guard to summon a carriage to take Jemal-Edin home to the Shchukin household again.

He went in a pleasant glow, hardly aware of the coach, the guards beside him, or the rain outside. But what was on his mind was not the czar's promises of future glories—but strudel . . . hot sweet strudel. He leaned back on the soft seats and thought about the empress. She was very lucky to come from a land where the food was so good. Someday he would go to Paris where the animal book had come from and he would see for himself elephants and tigers with great glaring eyes. And when he got home, he would show Feo how to play the new card game he had learned that afternoon.

The wife of the White Sultan, he decided, was a very wise woman, and most unusual. She told him she had nine children. He had never known a woman who lived long enough to have nine children. And like Feo's mama, she seemed to know as much as many men . . . but different things, and sometimes far more interesting. He wished his mother had known about books like that. She could have told him stories about animals and other countries . . . and how people in other countries traveled faster than a horse in things called trains. It seemed to him that women without veils were prettier than women with veils. And smarter, too. When he was allowed to go home again, he would discuss the matter with his father. There were so many good things about these Russians that his father had not told him.

He dreamed that night of the cozy study and the empress beside him, talking and smiling. And then in the dream the door opened and the czar came into the room. But suddenly it wasn't the czar looking down on them, but Shamil, and his eyes were glaring like the tiger's. The walls of the room slipped away, and he was alone and exposed to the wrath of Shamil!

"The world is carrion and he who seeks it a vulture!" he could hear his father roar as he had so many times before.

"But Father—you sent me here!" He cried out in his sleep and awoke to find he was trembling from fear, and sweating in his woolen nightshirt. Beside him in the dark, Saidia stirred and nuzzled his face, gave him a comforting lick and settled back to sleep. But Jemal-Edin lay awake, staring at the icon, thinking.

Had Shamil known when he sent him off as a hostage where his son was going? He had said Tchirkei, Jemal-Edin remembered. But he also remembered his father's hatred for the chieftain of the Tchirkei and their whole tribe. It did not seem likely that Shamil would willingly let him be taken to that village. Had he lied to him to make his going easier? For the first time he wondered, had he refused to go that awful afternoon, would Shamil have forced him to go—to save his life and pride? Especially his pride.

Jemal-Edin remembered a story he had heard once about his father, a story that was not meant for his ears. The old man who told it said that when Shamil was a boy, he had been unbearably proud and arrogant. So much so that the other boys of his village came to find him insufferable. One day the other boys set upon him and beat him until Shamil was nearly dead, then stabbed him for good measure. When they were gone, too proud to ask for help he had dragged himself away, up into the hills. There an old shepherd found him and cared for him until he recovered. Shamil stayed with the shepherd and trained himself until he could run faster and longer than any other man, lift the heaviest weight, ride the wildest stallion, cleave the thickest tree with his saber. He stayed away from Gimri for more than two years. When he returned, so the old man said, as Shamil's strength had grown, so had his pride and the respect he demanded. But now there was no one, man or boy, who dared challenge him and expect to live. And then, said the old man, Shamil saw that only holy men were shown greater respect than warriors, and thus he began to study the Koran.

When the old man had finished his story, there had been appreciative chuckles of amusement from his cronies grouped around the well. Then one of them had seen Jemal-Edin listening and all had looked afraid. Jemal-Edin did not understand the cause of their fear. He had found the story about his father very interesting.

But now, far from that high village and several years older, for the first time he had a glimmer of vague understanding as to why the old men had both laughed and been afraid.

He did not even bother to say good-bye to me, Jemal-Edin thought, remembering. When I was ready to go he kissed me and walked out to the mosque. As if once he could be sure I was going and his precious pride was saved, he didn't really care what would happen to me . . . so long as it saved him. . . .

"I will show him!"

He was still awake when the Shchukin coach rumbled into the courtyard at three that morning, bringing Mama home from her dinner party. As though released from the maze of his thoughts by the sound of the coach wheels, he sighed and slipped into sleep.

But from that night on he never dreamed of his father again.

AUTUMN FADED QUICKLY. THE GROUND FROZE AND THE last of the ducks left the pool in the park.

"As soon as the ice freezes solid we will go skating," Feo promised one morning when he had wakened early enough to join his friend riding.

"Yes?" said Jemal-Edin hesitantly. "What is skating?"

He soon learned. When they got back to the house Feo hurried him upstairs and showed him the skates that clamped onto one's boots and were strapped to hold them secure.

"If you are going skating, I am, too," Sophia announced and went off to hunt up her own skates.

"But the ice is not thick enough," Feo reminded her.

"Then why do we have our skates out?"

"To show Jemal-Edin."

"Oh."

"I did not know skating," explained Jemal-Edin. "Our brother is very kindly explaining it to me."

"It is very easy," Sophia assured him. "It's just like dancing, only faster and more fun. I can waltz on skates. Can you?"

"I fear not," said Jemal-Edin. "What is waltzing?"

"Like this." She took his hands in hers. "You put your feet together like this, then step sideways . . ."

"Sophia, I was going to show him how to skate," Feo protested.

"You cannot skate on the rugs. Mama would be angry. Besides, he must learn to dance, too, and this is as good a time as any. And this way they will not have so much to teach you when you start school at the palace, Jemal-Edin. Mama's maid Marie taught me. Marie says she is the finest dancer in the house, and I believe her!"

Although his father had never approved of such levity, dancing was not new to Jemal-Edin but the waltz was. To Sophia's delight he watched her very closely and then repeated her movements exactly. Feo, to keep from being left out, joined the game and learned to waltz almost in spite of himself.

"Now we will dance to the orchestra," said Sophia when the boys could move without tripping over their feet. She went to the music box on the bureau and turned the crank until the spring mechanism was wound tight, then pushed the button. The punched metal disk rotated over the pins to produce the hurried metallic notes of a Viennese waltz.

"That is much too fast," complained Feo.

"The faster you dance the sooner you will learn,"

she said somewhat illogically. "Besides, it will slow down soon anyhow."

So they danced, moving like berserk marionettes about the room. They wound the music box again and again until they were tired, and then let the spring unwind and the music slow to distortion, as did their steps. When finally the tinkling music stopped all three fell limply to the carpet like discarded puppets.

"If skating is more fun than this," Jemal-Edin said graciously to his little teacher, "I must learn quickly how to skate."

But skating turned out to be something quite different. On the first day Ivan pronounced the pond frozen and safe, and had the snow shoveled from its surface, the three children hurried out to play. Feo and Sophia strapped on their skates and, impatient to skate after so long a time as summer, sped off leaving Jemal-Edin to try to follow them.

He had some difficulty standing up. The edges of the skates seemed a thin surface on which to balance. But he managed. Then he took one step, a normal step. His feet slid out from under him with frightening speed and he fell hard, landing on his left hip and head. It was all he could do to keep from crying from the shock and pain, to say nothing of the humiliation.

Sitting up on the ice he waited until the bright spots of light quit bursting in his head. Then he attempted to stand again. Before he could get fully erect the treacherous skates betrayed him once more, and he went sprawling. This time he was more prepared for the fall and merely bruised one palm and both knees, and bit his tongue.

Ivan, who had been watching from a polite distance, now came over to Jemal-Edin and stuck out his hand. "An old fellow like me takes no chances on ice. My hobnailed boots will not let me slip. You stand up here now and try walking around me in circles until you get the feel of the ice under you."

"I have already felt the ice under me," said Jemal-Edin sitting where he fell. "It is very hard! I do not care for this game."

"Everyone falls at first," Ivan assured him. "But what others have learned to do, you can learn. Did you not get thrown from your horse when you first learned to ride?"

"Never!"

"Ah . . . well . . . perhaps you had more feeling for horses. But that is no excuse. Now take my hand and we will get you up off the cold ice."

Reluctantly the boy took the old man's hand and made a wobbly effort to stand erect. He was successful.

"Now, you will be the troika and I will be the horse," said Ivan. "Hang on!" Staying close to the edge of the ice, he pulled the boy along slowly.

"That looks like fun!" Sophia called and she skated up to watch. "Can I play, too?"

Jemal-Edin turned around to look at her and his sudden twist threw him off balance. Rather than fall himself, Ivan let go and Jemal-Edin came tumbling down on his rump again.

"You don't skate very well," Sophia observed. "You really should practice." With this remark she whirled away and cut circles across the ice to the other side of the pond. Jemal-Edin sat and watched her and on his face was a look of sheer disgust. Then, without getting up, he pushed himself across the ice, his pants and coat sweeping a shining path as he scooted. When he reached the bank of the pond, he took off his skates.

"I will come here when there is no one else to see me make a fool of myself!" he announced to Ivan. "When I skate with others, I will be better than they are—or I will not skate!"

It was an odd winter for the boy. Before, in the mountains, winter had been a time of misery, of retreat. Snow sealed the passes and nearly buried the villages. Wind and cold wet clouds penetrated the thickest woolens. All one could do was huddle on the mat before the smoky fireplace and try to pay attention to the aged mollah's endless teachings.

But here in St. Petersburg, where the supply of wood for the stoves in every room was unlimited, where the walls were thick and the windows double-paned, here winter was defied. The rooms were hotter than any summer he had ever known and dry as the desert.

These Russians seemed to welcome the snow. Even their bells sang of it. Through the damp air from the sea the chimes of the domed churches would ring out and be joined by the bells of the schools. There were bells on the oxen that pulled the merchants' sledges, bells on the troikas, bells on sleighs that shivered and tinkled like silvered glass, bells on taxis and coaches, bells on riding horses. Bells were everywhere!

In the afternoons, their lessons done, André and

Nanny would take the three children for a troika ride. Dressed in fur coats, gloves, boots, and hats, they would sit in the graceful sleigh, covered by fur rugs, and join the rest of the elite of the city out for their afternoon constitutionals.

Although there were parts of the great city where people suffered through these northern winters in greater misery than Jemal-Edin had ever known in his mountains, he did not see this or know it existed. The city Jemal-Edin saw was one of great comfort, wealth, and beauty, the world of the aristocracy.

In the hotels, bazaars, and shops along the Nevsky Prospect people and goods from all over the world were displayed for his eager eyes. Shop windows glowed with brass and silver samovars, gems and precious jewelry, porcelains from England, France, and China, carpets from Persia, and furs from the New World. And if the sight of all this luxury made him hungry, on the street corners vendors sold hot meat pies with flaky crusts that spurted steam and rich gravy when bitten into. There were cakes stuffed with cheese and dried fruit, and oceans of hot sweet tea to wash them down.

And while he munched in the warmth of his furs, he could watch the passing parade of imperial coaches mounted on runners for the winter, private sleighs and coaches painted in the colors of the families to whom they belonged, rich yellows and blues, golds, and ivory with lavender. Their coachmen wore the livery of their house, and the lucky passengers were wrapped in furs and comfort.

With the temperature as cold as twenty below, the

Neva River froze thick ice from bank to bank. The
snow was shoveled off the ice for a dozen different
skating rinks, some of them quite elaborate and outlined by gaily colored lanterns strung between poles.

Troops of a dozen different regiments of the czar
drilled and marched upon the frozen river, their uniforms making bright patches of color against the
white background. Troikas and sleighs raced over the
ice, the horses' breaths steaming in the freezing air. In
one big inlet Laplanders, their reindeers with them,
set up camp each winter to sell their furs. The Lapps
built cooking fires on the ice and drilled beneath it to
fish, as at home in their hide tents in St. Petersburg as
they were in the wasteland to the northwest.

While Feo and Sophia never seemed to stop chat-
tering on these rides, Jemal-Edin seldom spoke. There
was too much to see to waste time in discussing
things. In order to see even more, he would kneel on
the leather seat facing backward and watch the traffic
flow in their wake and the palaces and churches fall
into his line of sight. Occasionally something would
particularly impress him, and his mouth would fall
open in awe, until he recalled Nanny's admonition
about open mouths, and then he would cover his with
a mittened hand.

When the coals in the cast iron foot warmer began
to cool, and the wind and often falling snow had
chilled the occupants of the troika, when the driver
turned toward home once again, Jemal-Edin would
sink back onto the seat, allow himself to be covered to
his neck in furs, and sigh with satisfaction. What the
sultan with the emerald had told him so long ago was

true; he was seeing many wondrous things. And he did like it! Very much!

As each new day pushed the boy's past more firmly into the background, as he grew sure of himself, his whole manner slowly changed. Like a bud tightly gripped by winter, he was touched by the springlike warmth of affection from people who could literally give him almost anything in their world.

Made the emperor's ward and appointed by Nicholas a Coronet Prince, befriended by Feo and Sophia, Ivan, and all the household staff, loved by Nanny, carefully considered by Mama and Papa, taught by André, owner of his own horse and dog; Jemal-Edin for the first time felt himself a person in his own right. He was no longer merely the first-born son of Shamil Imam. He unwound from his protective sheath of silence, stretched in the new warmth and freedom, and began to grow.

BELOW THE PALACE WINDOW THE NEVA, RIPPLED BY THE incoming tide, reflected in distorted images the Greek and Italianate façades of the buildings lining its banks. The late-setting sun of the far north sent rays splaying above a bank of clouds over Finland. Homecoming gulls sailed out toward the gulf, their bodies flashing pink-white as they circled high overhead.

From the Customs House near the English quay men emerged and boarded a rowboat that would carry them out to Kronstadt to meet an incoming vessel. The streets of the city were still full of people; carriages rumbled along the parallel planks in the center of the cobblestone boulevards and racing cabs jolted past them, the bearded drivers exhorting their teams with whips and shouts.

Gilded onion-domes on a convent glowed in the sunset, and the turrets and spires and gaily painted rooftops of the skyline stood out in relief against the flat horizon. The spire of St. Nicholas gleamed as did the equestrian statue of Peter the Great overlooking the harbor.

As he looked out from the balcony window of his room, something in the peaceful scene below reminded Jemal-Edin of another summer, another sunset. Was it last year? It seemed a lifetime past, a world ago. When he rode down the path from Dargo, he thought, only Allah knew his journey would take him so far. And the others, his mother and brother, Javaret and her baby—had their journeys ended?

Thinking back to that time the view below lost focus and he was seeing not the city but Akhulgo and its surrounding mountains. In spite of the warmth of the evening he suddenly shuddered as if an icy mountain wind had chilled him.

"You better quit daydreaming and finish dressing." Feo's voice broke into his reverie. "We have to . . . What is it? Why do you look so sad?"

"Nothing . . ." Jemal-Edin shook his head and shrugged, embarrassed to be caught brooding. "Nothing," he repeated more firmly. "I was only thinking that . . . sometimes I hate balls." He struggled to fasten the golden frog clasps down the front of his dress uniform. "It is just like being in class all night— only His Majesty is my tutor."

"Father says the emperor's fondness for you makes you the envy of every man there." Feo paused to consider that thought. "But I don't think you're so lucky. You should do what I do." He pulled down his coat and polished some fingermarks off the shiny surface of his dress sword. "I always go up to the third floor and look at the cows. I wonder if they don't get tired of being up there? They have windows to look out of, but wouldn't you think sometimes they might enjoy walking in a pasture? At Kaluga when they let the cows out in the spring they run and frisk; it makes them very happy."

Out of courtesy to Feo, Jemal-Edin considered this abrupt change of subject. He knew very little about cows and cared even less. "Perhaps the cows like it?" he suggested. "After all, they are always warm and dry. All they have to do is eat and give milk to the servants . . . How did they get up there on the third floor?"

Feo shrugged. "I don't know . . . perhaps they were carried up when they were calves and let grow?"

"Well, anyway, I suppose cows are just as good company as some of the courtiers," decided Jemal-Edin. "But I can always tell when you've been sitting with them—your uniform smells of hay. Do I have everything on straight?"

Feo looked up from his polishing to consider his friend's appearance. Jemal-Edin was dressed, at the emperor's orders, in the court tailor's version of the native uniform of Daghestan—all in white velvet trimmed in gold braid with twin bandoleers of mock gold bullets slung across his shoulders. On his head was a tall white fur hat with gold visor and chin strap. At his waist was a gold belt with a little curved gold dagger. Jemal-Edin's real dagger did not match the tailor's idea of what was fitting.

After looking him over, Feo gave a mock sigh. "You are perfectly lovely!" he said with a sweeping bow. "May I have this dance?"

"Go dance with one of your cows," said Jemal-Edin. "I wish I could just wear my page's uniform like you."

"Gentlemen," a court lackey appeared in the open doorway of the boys' room, "His Majesty is nearly ready. Would you be so kind as to convene at his suite?" It was an order, not a request, and the two boys understood it as such.

To have one's son be appointed a member of the palace page corps was an honor eagerly sought by many noble fathers. It meant not only added prestige for the father, but instant social acceptance for the boy. With it came admittance to the Imperial Cadets, the most exclusive military academy from which the emperor's favorite officers almost invariably came, and most important, a thorough education in protocol and power. It was, however, an honor not always appreciated by the boys themselves.

In the hallway outside the emperor's rooms the bulk of his retinue awaited. All wore the formal dress uniform of their individual regiments; all had their hair cut neatly short. None wore beards and only those with dark hair were allowed to wear a small mustache—by imperial decree. And none of them smoked while they waited. Nicholas I hated the scent of tobacco smoke. Any officer who made the mistake of lighting a cigar in the royal presence ran the risk of seeing more of Russia's primitive outposts than he really wanted to.

Hardly had the announcement "Gentlemen, His

Imperial Majesty" been made than Nicholas strode through the door and the waiting men fell into line behind him. Jemal-Edin and Feo walked flanking the august presence, but several respectful paces behind.

Jemal-Edin had been feeling sorry for himself at being forced to wear his absurd white velvet, but he felt even greater sympathy for the empress' pages when she joined the retinue. To match the magnificent emeralds she wore with her white gown she had dressed the two small Nubian boys who carried her train in emerald green velvet with matching turbans. Long white ostrich plumes fluttered dizzily above and around their faces.

The grand entrance was made into a ballroom decorated as a summer garden. In one corner a waterfall splashed down over a mossy rock garden. Masses of tubbed roses surrounded fountains sparkling in the light of the chandeliers, light reflected back and back again by the mirrors lining walls and pillars. Against the heat from the guests and the thousands of wax candles, servant-powered fans whisked air across vats of colored ice concealed from view by tubs of potted ferns whose fronds dripped moisture in the steamy air. The fact that St. Petersburg had been wrought from a mosquito-laden swamp could not be forgotten on a warm summer night.

Good manners decreed that the heat be ignored. After the royal couple opened the dance, the orchestra played endless mazurkas and waltzes and polonaises. Women wearing huge jeweled headdresses and heavy gowns of silk and velvet with long peacock trains danced with gentlemen and officers in tight-throated uniforms of colors ranging from sedate whites, blues, and greens to red and canary-yellow, soft pink and lavender.

From where he stood on the dais, Jemal-Edin looked over the assembly below him and decided he was dressed in one of the more conservative costumes of the evening. This was the part of the ball he liked best, being able to stand and watch. Each time he saw a new step he practiced it cautiously behind the emperor's chair until he had memorized it well enough to be able to teach it to Sophia. Since he had come to live at the palace he missed the little girl. It pleased him to think that in two days, when the royal family left on their yacht for a summer cruise, he and Feo would join the Shchukin family at their summer villa by the shore.

From the corner of his eye he saw an old woman in black get up from her chair at the very back of the dais and make her way around the greenery toward him. It was the same old woman he had first seen at the military review. Feo saw her at about the same time and stepped over to warn him. "Oh-oh," he whispered, "she's here again tonight."

"Why does she always try to talk to me?" asked Jemal-Edin. "At every ball but one . . . And the officers who whisk her away always give me such odd looks. Then they look to see if His Majesty is watching us."

"She likes you," said Feo. "If you will excuse me, I think I will go off and see the cows now. His Majesty never misses me."

"Please stay . . ." But Feo had slipped behind a huge flowering tree and disappeared.

A talonlike hand fastened itself around Jemal-

Edin's right wrist. For a woman who looked so old, she was surprisingly strong. He turned, knowing who he was going to see and dreading it.

The old woman wasn't much taller than he was and, unlike the rest of the women in the court who sat up here, she never wore jewels. But there was an air of ferocious authority about her. She did not speak until she had spent several long moments searching his face like a hawk scanning a field for helpless rodents. Only the great respect for the aged which Fatimat had taught him kept him from rudely pulling away from her grasp.

"Beautiful boy!" she announced in broken Russian. "Beautiful boy! They treat you good?"

"Yes, madame," he said politely.

"You say 'Your Majesty,' " she said in reprimand, "I tell you that only once."

"Yes, Your Majesty."

A chamberlain who had been watching the pair from a distance stepped closer. The old woman deliberately turned her back on the man and, still clutching Jemal-Edin by the wrist, led him off into a more secluded corner.

"You are son of Shamil the Avar," she said in the Avarian tongue. Her mastery of this language was no better than her Russian, but her knowledge of it did surprise him. "They hold you here prisoner just as they hold me?"

"I am not a prisoner," objected Jemal-Edin.

"You are!" she insisted. "You just as I. For twenty years they keep me in convent—but I am still prisoner. Prisoner with fine clothes is still prisoner. Once

I had fine clothes—jewels . . ." She scanned his face again. "You believe me?"

Jemal-Edin nodded obediently, mentally noting that she had a distinct mustache and her mouth looked as if her lips had been stitched on too tight.

"Yes!" she nodded vigorously. "I was queen! No more. I am no queen here. I am prisoner!"

She looked about as though wary of being over-heard. "They take my kingdom. You know that? Just as they try to take your father's kingdom! I fought them—just like him. You know that?" Her head began to nod again at an old memory, until it rocked faster and faster as though she had lost control of it. "I fight them! I make them pay! I butchered czar's officers—just like he butchered my kingdom!" She smiled with an old satisfaction. "They thought I was only woman. But I show them. I was queen!"

Jemal-Edin shifted uncomfortably. She ignored him.

"Yes!" The head was nodding again, the high hawk nose drawn narrow. "They put me in chains! Yes! They march me across all Russia! Yes! But I am still queen!"

"Yes, Your Majesty."

She shot him a glance to see if he was mocking her. "You must be careful!" The talons shot out, gripped his chin and twisted his face close to hers so that she might fix his eyes more securely. Her breath was faintly fetid. "You are too young. They will make you forget. Forget your people. Forget mountains. You will laugh and dance and wear gold braid. But slave in gold braid is still slave!"

"Please! You are hurting me!" Half afraid of her now, Jemal-Edin pried her hand off his chin.

"Your Majesty, you must not overtax yourself," said a man's voice behind them in Russian. The chamberlain whom Jemal-Edin did not know bowed to the old woman, then to him. "You will excuse us, Prince Jemal-Edin. Her Majesty does not realize the limitations of her strength. It is time she retired for the night."

The old woman looked up at the man with cold hatred in her eyes. "May the wolves of winter eat your face!"

Jemal-Edin bit his lip to keep from laughing.

"He is jailer, this fop. That one of noble birth should sink so low, even with fancy title, tells you what to expect from Russia." The old woman spat on the leg of the man's immaculate white uniform.

"Perhaps you should return to the dais?" the chamberlain suggested to Jemal-Edin.

"Yes, sir!" the boy agreed gratefully. "Thank you, sir." Then remembering his manners, he bowed to the old woman and said, "Madame," before escaping back to his post. There was something evil about her. He had not had any nightmares in a long time, but somehow he was sure that if he listened to her for very long, they would return.

In Jemal-Edin's absence the emperor had returned and sat watching the czarina dancing below. Several nobles attempted to engage him in conversation, but he waved them away as if they were troublesome flies. At the sound of the boy's boots pounding up the steps he half turned to see who it was. Jemal-Edin instantly slowed to a sedate walk, but Nicholas crooked a finger at him.

"Sire?" said the boy, expecting a reprimand.

"I saw you having a little chat with one of my guests," said the czar. "What did she tell you?"

Jemal-Edin frowned, trying to recall all she had said, then blurted out the first thing that came to mind. "She said you marched her in chains across Russia for killing one of your officers . . ." He came to a confused halt, suspecting that one did not remind an emperor of things like that.

"Did you believe her?"

"I don't know, Sire. She seems a little . . ." He hunted for the correct word. If she were a queen, one did not call a queen crazy. "She frightened me," he said finally.

"Wise boy," said the emperor. "She was once a very frightening person. And what she said was the truth. But it was not *I* who made her walk in chains. I would not have been so lenient."

"She said she was a queen—and she could speak the language of the Avars," said Jemal-Edin, tactfully hunting for information.

"Which reminds me," the emperor ignored the ploy, "you are to be complimented on your linguistic ability. Your Russian and French are excellent now— after so short a time. We are very pleased. Your German, of course, needs polishing, as does your English, but that will come in due time, I am sure."

"Thank you, Sire," Jemal-Edin bowed and understood the subject of the old woman was closed. "I am determined to learn all I can."

"So your instructors tell me." The emperor smiled at his ward. "You may rest assured I shall help you in every way possible. You are young yet, but you show great promise. It is the same with Russia."

Having mentioned his favorite topic of conversation, he shifted in his chair to sweep his hand toward the dancers whirling before him. "In this room tonight are men from more than thirty different kingdoms. They speak twice that many languages and dialects and have a thousand different native customs. Yet all are Russians. As you are. Because you serve me, The Unity That is Russia.

"When the rulers and so-called intellectuals of Europe wish to reduce Russia to what they consider her proper place in the social sphere of world power, they refer to Russians as 'orientals' with a 'genius for adaptability'—as though by this phrase which they consider quite damning, we can somehow be dismissed. Yet they tremble and quake each time my armies march! They accuse us of copying everything and creating nothing. Yet we will create an empire, the greatest the world has ever seen!"

The emperor looked into the bright eyes watching his face as he spoke. "You will not understand all I say as yet, Jemal-Edin," he conceded, "but you will be an important part of it. You will help me to achieve my dream. You will someday take back this dream of unity to your own people. You will make the Caucasus part of Russia!"

"I would like that, I think," said Jemal-Edin. "But before I return to Daghestan, I would like to see the rest of the world, visit all the places in the pictures in my books!"

Nicholas permitted himself a slight smile. "Like good soldiers, we, each of us, must do what duty demands. The day will come when you will see some of the things of which you dream. But I have already seen most of them—and I tell you there is nothing in the rest of the world, short of scenery, that you cannot find in St. Petersburg. And most of it is within my palaces."

"It is indeed a place of wonders, Sire," Jemal-Edin agreed fervently. "Like the palace of the greatest djinn!"

"And this djinn does not disappear in a puff of smoke back into a golden lamp," laughed Nicholas, pleased by the comparison.

"Now you must excuse me. I must put to rest some of the envy our little tête-à-tête has caused in the noble hearts of equally noble subjects. But you remember what I told you, Prince Jemal-Edin. Some day I shall need you, Russia shall need you. As will your native land. We want you well prepared for that day. I believe and trust you will not disappoint us."

"I shall try not to, Sire." Jemal-Edin bowed as the czar rose. He watched the tall figure of the emperor walk down the steps and drift across the ballroom, men bowing, women curtsying before him. Something about the scene reminded him of Shamil's progression through a village square. For a moment

Jemal-Edin tried to imagine Shamil here, walking into a ballroom such as this, or riding through St. Petersburg.

With a flash of intuition he saw a vivid picture of Shamil's face set with cold disapproval in abhorrence of this worldly place. "My father fights to keep Daghestan as it was," he thought. "He wants nothing to change. He is fighting to keep the past. Like the old queen."

And by the same intuition he knew then that he could no longer accept that past, that he himself had changed. He wanted the future Russia offered, that Nicholas offered. He felt very proud that such a man had faith in him. He would, he vowed, never disappoint him!

The orchestra broke into the strains of the newest waltz from Vienna. A murmur of gay approval swept through the crowd as if word of a new sugar source had reached a hive of happy bees. The dancers whirled and dipped and flashed. In the shadow of the czar's gilt chair, Jemal-Edin danced alone.

EPILOGUE

Jemal-Edin kept his promise. He never disappointed Nicholas. With the zeal of a convert, he became more Russian than any Grand Duke. As he grew older it sometimes must have seemed to the boy that his life in St. Petersburg was one long glorious party. For though he told others that he had forgotten his past, he had not. Nor was he to be allowed to. It was all still there, waiting, buried just below the surface glitter of those years.

At an age when most children are in kindergarten, he was learning guerrilla warfare. And after the fanatically harsh and Spartan discipline Shamil exacted, Jemal-Edin felt Nicholas's autocratic rule almost gentle. The czar was truly very fond of him and became more so as the years passed. The affection was mutual.

Jemal-Edin was an outstanding student. By the time he received his commission he spoke six languages, read classic Latin and Greek, knew botany

and astronomy, was a fair musician and a better art-
ist. He was a great favorite not only of the royal family but with the court in general. Much to the czar's
pleasure, the boy never got into the awkward scrapes
with dancing girls and wild parties as his sons, the
Grand Dukes, all too often did.

With his goal of governing Daghestan for Russia, of
opening his country to the rest of the world, Jemal-
Edin dreamed of taking back teachers and doctors, of
building roads and bridges, of freeing women from
the veil and educating them. Czar Nicholas appointed
both him and Feo as his aides-de-camp so that they
might learn government firsthand.

At eighteen he was six feet, four inches tall and
very handsome. He was gifted with both charm and
wit. This, combined with his always slightly sad
brown eyes and sweet smile made Coronet Prince,
Lieutenant Jemal-Edin Shamil a great favorite with
women of all ages. He fell in love with a noble Russian woman and they asked the czar's permission to
marry. Nicholas refused. Jemal-Edin must remember
his duty and make a politically wise marriage to a
Daghestani woman upon his return there.

But aside from that one personal grief, it was as if
destiny had chosen to compensate him for the de-
privation and tragedy of his childhood.

The long glorious party ended abruptly when
Jemal-Edin was twenty-four. Shamil, who had never
forgotten his first-born son, or forgiven the Russians
for taking him so far away, decided to wreak vengeance on his enemies. He knew Jemal-Edin was the
czar's great favorite. Accordingly, Shamil had kid-

209

napped two Georgian princesses and their children, subjected them to great misery, and held them as hostages against the return of Jemal-Edin.

At first the czar refused. Months passed in fruitless negotiations for the princesses' release. The czar's armies were dying in the Crimea. He had little time or interest now in Shamil or Georgian princesses. But pressure was applied at court. Finally, in desperation, Nicholas I recalled Jemal-Edin from his post at Warsaw and advised him of the situation. Jemal-Edin volunteered to return at once to the Caucasus. It was, he said, his duty. Only he could guess the true condition in which these hostages were existing.

For the last time he knelt before the czar; Nicholas blessed him, and both men wept as they said good-bye. Two weeks after Jemal-Edin left on the trip south that winter, Nicholas I was dead of pneumonia and despair as his dreams for Russia mired in the mud of the Crimea. On the day the hostage exchange took place beside a wild river near the Georgian border, Nicholas I was buried in St. Petersburg. Jemal-Edin's grief was equalled only by Shamil's jubilation.

But Shamil's joy at his son's return was short-lived. He quickly decided he was disappointed in the exchange. This tall young stranger with the elegant manners could quote the Infidels' Bible as easily as the Koran. He was not the obedient boy Shamil had sent down the path from Akhulgo. "I gave them an Avar. They have betrayed me again! They sent me back a Russian!" he complained.

The "Russian" had returned with a crystal chandelier in his luggage, the gift he had long ago wished to bring his mother. Now he learned Fatimat had grown ill and died almost ten years before. She would never see the crystals sparkle with candlelight. Javaret, too, was dead; she and her infant son were shot by snipers as they attempted to escape with Shamil from Akhulgo the day after Jemal-Edin was taken hostage. Upon being told this news, Jemal-Edin wept openly. To Shamil such public grief was both unseemly and a sign of weakness. An Avar does not cry.

Along with Hassan and the older men on his staff, Shamil distrusted this Russian son—all the more so because of Jemal-Edin's influence on Kazi Mohammed. After long years of separation, Kazi Mohammed still appeared to worship his older brother. He, along with the other young warriors, could not hear enough of Jemal-Edin's exciting talk of ballrooms and unveiled women, wine and dinners, bright lights and cities, railroads and telegraphs and steamships, all the world they had never seen or even heard of before.

In time Hassan and the other Naibs convinced Shamil that this worldly talk would corrupt the morality of his warriors. Shamil agreed. He had initially taken from Jemal-Edin all his personal "Russian" possessions, his music box, his sketching pads, his books and pictures. Now, to satisfy his nobles, Shamil once again sacrificed his first-born son.

Jemal-Edin was put under house arrest; the young warriors were forbidden to speak with him. The young man passed the days sitting on the roof, or out riding, and always looking longingly toward the north, toward Russia—toward home. The guards reported this to Shamil. What was there, they wondered, that he missed it so much?

Shamil then ordered Jemal-Edin sent to an almost deserted village in the highest and most remote peaks of the Caucasus where only an ancient Tartar dialect was spoken.

Here, his door guarded by men with whom he could not communicate, made weak by the altitude, kept in solitary confinement in an unheated hut for more than a year, Jemal-Edin was stricken with tuberculosis. Here he died, alone, on a summer night in 1858.

One year and one month later, Shamil surrendered.

BIBLIOGRAPHY

✳ *Books*

BLANCH, LESLEY. *The Sabres of Paradise*. New York: The Viking Press, 1960.

CUSTINE, MARQUIS DE. *Journey for Our Time*. Edited and translated by Phyllis Kohley. New York: Pellegrini and Cudahy, 1951. (This is an abridged translation of the Marquis de Custine's classic "La Russie in 1839," first published in Paris in 1843.

GRZIMEK, BERNHARD. *Wild Animal, White Man*. Translated from the German by Michael Glenny. New York: Hill & Wang, 1966. Copyright held by several German magazine publishers and newspapers.

WRIGHT, LAWRENCE. *Clean & Decent*. New York: The Viking Press, 1960.

✳ *Encyclopedias*

Encyclopedia Americana. 1961.

Encyclopedia Britannica. 1972.